AKASHIC URBAN SURREAL CLASSICS

DON DIMAIO OF LA PLATA

BY ROBERT ARELLANO

AKASHIC BOOKS
NEW YORK

This is a work of satirical fiction. Although it contains caricatures that parody public figures from a real and recent racketeering scandal, all names, characters, places, and incidents are the product of the author's corrupt imagination.

Published by Akashic Books
©2004 Robert Arellano
Layout by Sohrab Habibion
Illustrations by William Schaff

ISBN: 1-888451-51-3
Library of Congress Control Number: 2003109539
All rights reserved
First printing
Printed in Canada

Akashic Books
PO Box 1456
New York, NY 10009
Akashic7@aol.com
www.akashicbooks.com

DEDICATED TO

SYLVIA MORSE, DUCHESS OF COBBLE HEDGE,
MARQUESA OF EDGEWOOD,
LADY OF CRANSTON AND ENVIRONS.

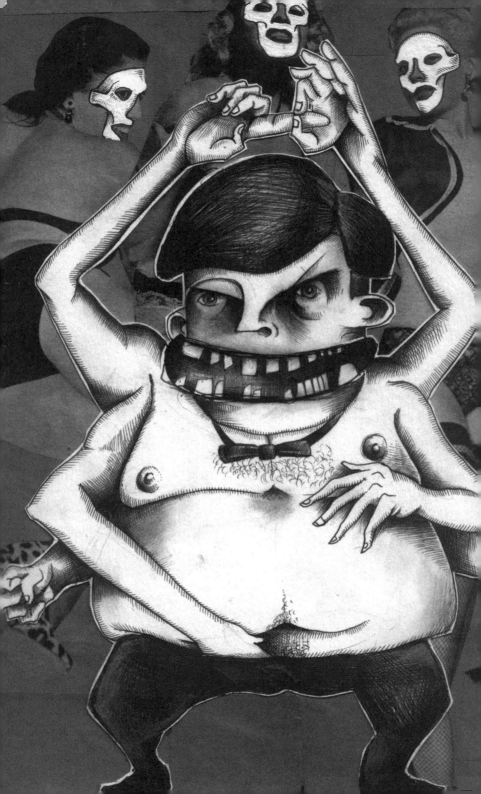

FART I: *Which treats of the station in life and the pursuits of the famous 'gina man, Don Dimaio of La Plata.*

In a village of La Plata, the name of which I have no desire to recall, there lived not so long ago one of those 'gina men who always halve their pants in a whack, with ancient cockles, a skinny frank, and a gay hand for the chafe.

BRAUTWAY, SATURDAY, 7:00 PM

S ANCHEZ muscles through traffic to Noel's on the West Side. At the academy, his bicep was the biggest in the class. "Dong forgay to cling up joo face, jorona."

"Eat shit, bean-eater."

The car crawls up on the curb and I see through the window Cantare is already working the room. *"Brautway Business Association"* reads the itinerary. *"Mid-tier contributors, ten minutes."* I won't even give them that. Hank has already done the groundwork and this crowd is more motivated by aloof Dimaio. Such is the big-town businessman's small-time ego. Give them too much attention and they're liable to hold back in the final drive. Keep them begging for scraps like new sidewalks and the contributions come pouring in.

I pull the mirror out of the seatback pocket to clean up my face and adjust the rug. I reflect on the arm rest. I decide I'll wait for Cantare and take a swallow of cognac from my flask instead. I stub out my cigarette, Sanchez opens the door, and tongue-tied Tommy Fritos extends a sweaty hand from the curb. "Hey! Mayor!"

"How are you, Tommy?"

"Fine. Nice you come to our shindig, Mayor. Da BBA connibyoo fie tousand today."

"That's terrific, Tommy. It's a very important campaign and this fundraiser is a great kickoff."

Fritos, a Portaguee who's bought himself out of a couple of back-tax scraps via Cantare, shadows me to the entrance. "Always funraise, Pally! You just win, now you funraise again!" "Can't start too early getting ready for the next race. I'm going to be the longest-serving mayor in the history of La Plata. And what's good for the city is good for you, Tommy." "I no complain, Mayor." He stops in the doorway. "I just hope you put inna good word for me onna schools lease." Son of a bitch cod-eater, always fishing for favors. Fritos has no sense of finesse. Seen too many movies about Godzilla and gangsters.

"Excuse me, Tommy. Don't you think it's time we went inside so I can address our guests?" I push past him into the restaurant and a hundred or so local businessmen all quit working on their hundred-dollar rubber chickens to give up the standing applause. Sanchez has pulled the portable podium out of the trunk of the car and set it up in front of the bar. The seal of the city is stained with a splotch of ketchup, a leftover from this afternoon's Mount Govern neighborhood picnic. Cantare hands me a B&D on the rocks.

"Thank you for coming. I'm especially grateful for your generous contributions to Pals of Pally. Many of you have met my campaign treasurer and director of administration, Hank Cantare. You're the ones feeling for your wallets. Heh heh."

Here's what my speech would sound like if the gathered shitforbrains had a subliminal interpreter:

"Brautway is not just a beautiful street with a rich history in our fair city. *Brautway is not just a desolate strip amputated from the heart of the city when they built the interstate.* It's a vital commercial-residential neighborhood of hard-working businessmen such as yourselves supplying much-needed goods and services to a diverse mix of decent citizens. *It's a burnt-out industrial zone of vultures who prey on the miscreants of mongrel races forced together by poverty.* For your industry and civic pride, I salute you. *For sticking it to them with inferior product at exorbitant mark-ups, here's a one-finger salute.* We're all in this together. *Except you do it for chump change compared to most of the rackets I might deem worthwhile.* I look forward to leading the progress of the Brautway neighborhood. *I look the other way while your buildings crumble and residents become ever more desperate.* Now if you'll pardon me, I have to attend the wake of a retired police officer, one of La Plata's finest. *Excuse me while I use your campaign contributions to go powder my nose.* And don't forget to tell the wife to pick up a jar of Dimaio's Own Mayonnaise at the market—all profits go to charity. *My favorite charity.*"

The suckers eat it up. Applause, firm handshakes around the front five tables while I pull Cantare toward the exit. Have to use every opportunity to plan the campaign, so I'm taking my director of administration along for a car conference. At the door, Fritos hands me one of those putrid Lisbon cigars he's always pushing on people. I slip the stinker in my breast pocket, giving the hanky a squeeze to absorb the chourice grease. Sanchez opens the car door and I shove Cantare in back, climbing in behind. Sanchez gets in front, auto-lock goes *ka-thunk,* and in two seconds we've left the BBA in the dust.

"Whey nex, jorona?"

Itinerary reads, *"Taxidermists Convention, Natural History Museum."*

"Take us to William Rogers Park."

Cantare says, "Whatcha got, boss?" I open the armrest compartment and pull out a twenty-dollar bill twisted into a fat pony pack. Cantare gently works open the triple fold, dips his fingertip in the dust, and rubs a little on his gum. The effect makes Cantare's jaw drop better than if I showed him a check for ten grand made out to the campaign and signed *Steinem.* "Mother of God! Is there more?"

"Try it. Make sure you like it."

"Oh, I like, all right!"

I pull out the mirror and pour a little pile. Sanchez is running reds, swerving over the double yellow. "Easy on the curves, pen-day-ho!"

"Careful with that, Pally," Cantare says. "You might lose some in the crack between the plastic and the glass."

"Don't be a Jew, Hank. There's always more where this came from."

I hand Cantare the mirror and a credit card from my clip. Hank starts chopping, taking his time. He gets as much pleasure out of the prep as from the effect. Of all the close associates I know I can collar for an impromptu strategy meeting, Hank Cantare is by far my favorite. Whether fundraising or hell-raising, he always does a thorough job.

Finally, two sets of five long, fine lines span the face of the mirror: bass and treble clef waiting for the music. Cantare flicks a C note from his clip, rolls it up tight and offers it to me. "Jorona?"

"You go ahead. I want to watch your expression."

I hold the mirror under Cantare's nose. He leans forward and pinches one nostril, sticks the rolled bill in the other, and huffs up a line. Hank barely pauses before attacking another and another and another, each time swiftly switching pinch and straw. Four deep snorts before he tosses his head back. Cantare's skull lolls against the headrest while his body melts over leather upholstery. Hank manages a moan: "Fuck."

"Not so shabby, right?"

Cantare tilts his head forward. His chin drops to his chest. Eyes like Greek olives dilate in adoration. "Black baby Jesus!"

"Okay, now can you pull your shit together enough to hold onto this?" When I pass Cantare the mirror he snaps to, grabbing the handle.

I travel a lot around this town, sometimes ten or twelve events a day, so the best place for recreation is the backseat. Everywhere I go, people know me the moment I walk in the door, and even in the john folks spot the shoes. When the mayor's wingtips poke out under the door of a stall, it doesn't take much imagination for a journalist with his dick in his hand glancing over his shoulder from the urinal to think he detects fairy dust on the leather toes. Posting Sanchez at the door of course just arouses suspicion. Sometimes at a fundraiser in somebody's home, where it's one-at-a-time and lock-the-door, I can straddle the throne and lay out a few lines on the porcelain top of the tank, as long as there aren't too many knickknacks to push out of the way, but even there you can't be sure the next guy's not some muckraking freak who'll take swab samples and conduct residue tests. Believe me, they're out there. So I do it in the car, La Plata's most famous sedan, numero uno on the plate, behind blacked-out windows, with the oval mirror I use to straighten my hair. Flask in the side pocket to take the edge off. Q-tips in the armrest to pluck out bloody boogers and shove them in with the butts in the ashtray Sanchez empties at anonymous gas stations. Besides my house, the backseat is the only place I can be alone.

Cantare, clutching the mirror in a corpse-stiff grip, says, "Fritos can come up with five for that schools lease."

"Five, huh?" It takes me a few extra breaths thanks to the asthma and forty-some years of smoking, but I manage to put away four lines like Hank's. "You tell Fritos ten or he can kiss my ass."

Cantare squints at me through the coke-glazed haze. "Ten grand?"

We're on Maplewood Ave. when I lift off. In the window of Donut Donkey, a poster of a Dusted Cruller reads: *"Enjoy the Fresh Powder."* Hell yes! "No, ten donuts, cruller-dick." Cantare starts laughing his ass off, his whole body shaking. I steady the mirror. "Don't spill that, you son of a bitch!" Two lines left.

I light up a cigarette and Sanchez pulls into the park. "Jorona, joo Juan I shoo go stray to de moosayum?"

"No! Hell no! First the zoo, then the museum. Go the long way, take the loop road."

"Zo? Zo's close, jorona. Pass dark."

"Shut up and drive."

High as satellites and flying right here on the ground, the hammer hits Sanchez sails us through the schizophrenic cyclorama that is William Rogers Park while Cantare and I bounce around in the backseat. We're clawing at armrests, faces pressed against the tinted windows, gawking at the historic shacks and bronze statues and taking turns describing them as they come alive. Betsy Rogers's cottage: That's the house where Dahmer lives. He's hacked up some kids to eat and is burying their bones out by the carousel. The pilgrim and the squaw· It's bloody Goldman holding butchered Nicole. O. J. has stalked off in the bushes wearing one iron glove. Poseidon with his trident: Geronimo holding the spear that stuck a thousand Texas Rangers. The Japanese garden is Hiroshima about to blow. The marble band shell is the Coliseum awash in Christian blood. Abe Lincoln looks so rigid because he's paralyzed, a fresh bullet in his spine.

"Goddamnit, Sanchez! Pull in here!"

Sanchez turns into the zoo parking lot and we coast across the painted grid. The lines are reminders, not just of the two on the mirror, but of the hill in the bill. There's a lot more left.

"Pull over near the ticket booths and get the watchman to call the zookeeper."

"Okay, jorona. Bah dong forgay to cling up joo face."

"Fuck you," I say.

"Yeah, fuck off," adds Cantare.

I grab Cantare's tie, wrap it up in my fist, and choke it tight against his throat, my heart pounding to get out of my chest. "Fuck *you*, Hank! I'm the only one who tells Sanchez fuck you!"

Cantare is sweating. "What the fuck, boss? I didn't mean nothing. Besides, I didn't say fuck you, I just told him to fuck off."

"Don't what-the-fuck me! I'm the only guy says fuck you or fuck off. And fuck off is a lot more serious than fuck you. I reserve fuck off for times when I'm really pissed, like I'm about to be with you if you don't shut the fuck up."

"What's the fucking difference between fuck you and fuck off?"

"Fuck you means fuck you. But fuck off means fuck you and on top of that go fuck yourself: Fuck off. I don't say fuck off to my friends and Sanchez is my fucking friend. For you to say fuck off to my friend is even worse than saying fuck you to me." I've got the knot of Cantare's tie in one hand. The other hand is holding the cigarette and Hank's wild eyes are fixed on the burning tip. It's quiet. I don't know how much time has passed since I finished shouting but I know it's been less than a second. The car is silent except for engine idling and heater blowing. There's condensation on the windows. Outside it's dark and cold, and here in the backseat I'm grinding my teeth while feeling the back of my throat delightfully rot away and I feel great. Hank's got both hands on the handle of the mirror like an altar boy holding a crumb catcher and I have to laugh. It hits Cantare at the same time. He starts cracking up, tears in his eyes. "Watch it, Hank! You'll spill it."

By the time we start settling down, Sanchez has his big arm on the seatback and a weary look in his eyes. "Jorona, joo Juan I shoo tell de gar to gay de zokipper, oh no?"

Cantare apes, *"Jorona, joo Juan I shoo tell de gar to gay de zokipper, oh no!"* More uproar. Fat tears spring from Cantare's eyes and mine. My cheeks hurt and I can hardly catch my breath.

Sanchez glares back at us, double-chin drooping across his massive shoulder. "Because ees standing outsie de weendo, jorona."

There's the guard, all right, a tree of a geek perched patiently at the driver's door. He knows my car. Everybody in La Plata does. But I can't be bothered by this looming loser of a rent-a-cop. I take a pull from the flask and enjoy a few more puffs of menthol before stubbing the butt and leveling my eyes on Sanchez. "Don't patronize me, ee-ho day poo-tah! Get that rent-a-pig to tell the mayor the zookeeper's here. I mean—you know what I mean!"

Sanchez powers his window down a crack and speaks to the watchman while Cantare holds the mirror and examines his reflection intensely. The guard trots off. "Zokipper coming, jorona. Shoobee jussa mini."

"What do you want to do with this?" Cantare says, meaning the last two lines. They're a little crookeder than the first eight we snorted but still full of velvety goodness.

"What do you call that?"

Another thing I love about Cantare, he gets hit with his little poetic fits. "That," says Hank, eyes sparkling, caps gleaming, "is what is known as Vanna's panty hose."

Cantare and I each go up one of Mrs. White's stockings. Our noses meet at the crotch.

"You hold onto the rest, Hank." Cantare expertly folds the bill back up and Sanchez opens the door. I get out of the car and Hank follows me to the gate. A beam of light comes bobbing down the path from the Plains of Africa and I wipe my nose on my sleeve just in time to greet the third-shift zookeeper. "Hello, Andy!"

"Good evening, Mayor. Back again to visit our new arrival?"

"Yup. I'd like to introduce him to a friend of mine. This is Hank Cantare, my director of administration."

"Nice to meet you, Mr. Cantare."

"Pleased to meet you. Call me Hank."

Andy unlatches the gate, pointing the flashlight at our feet. Cantare and I follow him back up the path. "I think our new boy could teach Hank something about fundraising, Andy."

"I bet you're right, Mayor."

Cantare starts pulling it together. "It's an important job you've got here, Andy, taking care of all the animals. How many are there in all?"

"About 700 hundred of more than 200 species of mammal—ten different kinds of primate, for instance—but when you count the birds, amphibians, and captive insects, the number of occupants gets into the tens of thousands."

"Wow!"

"Of course, I'm just one of a dozen keepers. I'm only here five nights from 9 until 6. You two are in charge of the real zoo." Cantare and I both oblige with a *heh heh*. "I'll run ahead and wake the baby, make sure mom's docile. You know the way, Mayor?"

"You bet, Andy."

"Here, take the flashlight."

"Hank and I will be right behind you. We'll try not to disturb any of the sleeping creatures." Andy scampers away.

Cantare says, "How do you do it, Pally, remembering everybody's names?"

"I told you before. It's mnemonics. Makes people happy."

"But everybody? I mean, for Christ's sake, the night zookeeper!"

"'Animal Andy.' How many favors big and small have you gotten simply for remembering someone's name?" I snap off the flashlight to soak in the night. Cantare rests a hand on my shoulder. "Eyes adjusting okay, Hank?"

"Can't see a goddamn thing."

We continue up the dark path. The rush of the nearby highway is drowned in the prehistoric music of La Plata wetlands: invisible crickets at their racket and murmuring toads who want to snack on those crackling wings. Our footfall, heavier than the soft-shoed zookeeper's, sends gobs of croaking monsters plop-plopping into the pond for refuge. This triggers the slumbering ducks, who shoosh from their beds in the reeds. Cantare says, "It sounds like summer here."

"Marsh country. It's like this year round. It used to be this way all over this part of the world before the cities came along."

The Arctic Ocean window looms midnight blue as we pass. Something blooms darkly in the glass for a second, spins, and disappears. The sea lion swims laps in this tank all night, making up fifty yards at a stretch for the million miles he'd migrate in his lifetime. I lead Cantare to the adjacent aquarium. He steps warily around the edge, staring into the dark depths. "What's it going to be, Pally? Barracuda? Shark?"

"Shut up. You'll see."

Andy has successfully coaxed the pup onto the poolside platform while his sedated mother hibernates in the den. I flip the switch in the wall of fake rock, bathing the baby in cool, electric moonlight. "My God!" says Hank, "he's a living teddy!"

"Hm," Andy says, "but he's already got the strength to rip a man's finger off. In a few months it will be an arm. Then we'll have to give him a shot before handling just like we do his mom."

"You know, Andy, if Hank could get people to contribute to my campaign the way this little guy's gotten donors to fork over to the zoo, I could buy national spots on all the major networks."

"What good would that do, Mayor? It's a local election."

"I'm not talking about mayor, Andy. I'm talking about president. Heh heh."

"Oh, boy! You'd win, too."

Squatting over the infant polar bear, Cantare's face gets a mothering look. "His fleece is white as snow."

Next, Andy gives us a tour of the primates. "Marmosets are from Central and South America. They've got claws instead of nails. And these fellows, the white-cheeked gibbons, are from Asia." While the rest of the tribe brood in fake trees in their tranquilized stupors, one gibbon fidgets on the lip of a stone basin. "We've got this guy sedated at the maximum dose but he still exhibits antisocial tendencies."

"Like what?"

"Aggression towards females. Frequent masturbation."

Cantare says, "Check out that crazy monkey!"

"Ape," says Andy.

"Huh?"

"Monkeys have tails. Apes do not. Gibbons have no tails, so they are not monkeys at all. They are apes."

"Where'd you say they come from?"

"Southeast Asia. But their natural habitat is rapidly dwindling due to overforestation."

"What's that mean?"

"It means when you're out shopping for furniture, don't buy tropical hardwoods."

Cantare says, "Oops."

"Hey, Andy, let's check in on the orangutans."

"You two go ahead, boss. I'd like to stay here for a minute." Andy and I head next door to Borneo and let Cantare linger with the gibbons.

"How's the wildlife treating you, Andy?"

"Love it, Mayor. In the brighter months I say good morning to as many of the diurnals as I can, and I always visit with the nocturnals. Some of them enjoy it when I give them a special feeding—throwing mice in the air for the owls, for instance.

Makes them feel like they're still hunting." Andy is one of those robust loners who don't see much daylight and stay at the job for the whole of their lives—and somehow, when they die, another nut who clearly wouldn't be suited for any other career comes along and replaces them. Sounds like fun, but it would drive any normal guy crazy after a few months.

"Hank! What the fuck are you doing!" Behind our backs, Cantare has climbed into the cage with the white-cheeked gibbons and now the whole colony is thrashing.

The irate ape cries, *"Ook ook! Ai ai ai!"* He springs off the edge of the stone basin, clawing Cantare across the face and bursting through the door. Andy drags Cantare out of the cage and slams the door shut before before the rest of the gibbons can tear him to bits. He scrambles around the primate area with the flashlight but the manic ape has escaped.

"I don't get it. They're pretty doped up most of the time. It's in the diet, like anthropoid Prozac." Andy's hand is trembling so bad I have to help him dial. He's never had to make this call, sounding the alarm to bring in the search team. "Otherwise they'd get too depressed about losing the life of the wild."

When the head zookeeper answers, Andy starts explaining the situation. He looks like he's about to faint so I grab the phone. "Charlie? It's Pally. Andy's not to blame, okay? Call Umbilico and tell him I said to put out an APB."

Chimp-face Charlie.

Back in the car, Hank holds an ice pack against a gash beneath his right eye and I take a long pull from the flask. Cantare's a good coagulator, but Andy told him he'd have to see a doctor for a tetanus shot. "That was so fucking stupid, Hank."

"All that blocks off the cage is a little piece of plywood, so I just slid it up. If those fuckers are so wild, shouldn't they have a lock on the pen?"

"They don't count on even the world's biggest fucking bozo trying to climb in during the day."

"Shitty little monkey."

"Ape."

"All right. Shitty fucking ape."

"Listen, Hank, you can't come to the reception looking like this. Give me back the coke. You don't want that on you in the emergency room."

"I don't have it," Cantare sniffs.

"Don't fuck with me. Give me the fucking coke."

"I gave it to the gibbon."

"What?"

"I let him have a taste and he grabbed the rest."

"The whole thing?"

"Took the twenty, too."

"You fuckhead! That was almost three grams!"

"I felt bad about the sideboard."

"What the fuck are you talking about?"

"It's a wedding present for my girlfriend. It's going to go in the dining room. Made in China."

"Are you fucking nuts? You don't give a gibbon coke!"

"I'll tell you one thing, the goddamn monkey liked it all right!"

After putting my shithead director of administration in a cab to the hospital, I have Sanchez drive me over to the Natural History Museum, but the taxidermy convention is strictly stuffed shirts and old birds. "Hey, where's the formaldehyde?" No booze, just beer and cheap wine. Fuck'em. In five minutes I'm back in the backseat.

A SHREW with more cleave than buttons on her, flopped teats for his evening feel, harlots for a Saturday, rentals on Friday, and a young stripper as a special delicacy for Sunday, went to account for three-quarters of his sin-come.

I-69, SATURDAY, 9:00 PM

ON the Eden Street offramp, horns are honking and engines are revving. Herds of limos, some of them buses, flank both shoulders of Adams Ave. Cars are rearing up on each other. It's Saturday night and all that steel and chrome is hungry for the curves of La Plata. The tires want to feel her road. Fenders want up in her alleys.

Here are the Darci Brothers—Perry, Onan, and Riley—making asses of themselves again. They're all dressed as turkeys and lined up on one of their overpriced sectionals. The fat one (by which I mean the fattest one: They're all fat) raises a knife to carve a cartoon Pilgrim and Indian tied-up and stretched-out on a serving platter, a speech bubble above their heads bearing the marketing cry made out of the Darcis' first names: *"PÉ ÖN RÌ!"* Next is Nash Naugayde, rooftop mascot for La Plata Pest Control. Kids look forward to this curve, peering out windows after those big, buggy eyes. When the Red Rat goes by, the child in every grown man goes "Hi." Here's one of my own. I look good two stories tall. They air-brushed in a light tan and feathered the edge where the toupee overlaps the ears. Of course I'm a shoe-in for reelection. The city has been renaissanced up the ass, my approval rating is in the high eighties, and the likelihood is I'll run unopposed, but that doesn't mean I don't need to campaign. Polling shows a little doubt among the Latino community, my bread-and-butter contributors, as to whether I can keep it up another term, so the printed message is simple and direct: "*CAN I? . . . CI!*" Fucking numbnuts at Pals for Pally can't even spell the wetback *yes.*

The way my billboard is situated in front of the pitchfork skyline turns me into La Plata's devilish doorman. Every guy for a hundred-mile radius knows this is the city for flesh exchange and in each one's filthy little mind I, Mayor Donald "Pally" Dimaio, am the pimping host.

"*Welcome to Pallywood!*" There's a black bowtie on my bare neck and a lecherous grin on my face. "Man, you look like you've got it made! Maybe you're a mobster, or a lawyer who practices his extortion over the table—either way, you've come to the right place to blow some ill-gotten gains."

All across the city are dirty storefronts with twenty-dollar half-hour massages where The Special is considered an obligatory extra fifty paid in private to the Asian ladies. Most guys are finished in less than five minutes. A halfway-decent, parlor pony ride will run you five bills easy, and then there's the doctors and crushed-pill pushers rich enough to bring a couple of strippers home or to a hotel for a private hump. A deep-in-debt dentist I know regularly drops ten grand taking three girls back to his office chairs and strapping them in for all-night nitrous parties. He's trying to cut down to once a month. Here in La Plata we've got bachelor-party Disneylands like Heaters and Club Fancies and bottom shelf establishments like Hunter's Cabin, the only thirty-dollar room in the smudgy heart of the city, where the hotel lobby happens to open onto an all-night strip club. Lapdance dens like the Velvet Puppet are legal as long as your pants stay on, and if you want to take them off there's always somebody you can pay who'll look the other way. The classy act is Crafty Beaver, with its so-called dressing rooms, where it's a thousand for a chilled bottle of Dom Perignon and it doesn't even come with a stripper, who'll run you at least another G, even more for the occasional guest porn star who'll provide a one-of-a-kind private session for a few moneyed fuckers who know the club password.

"You with the kite! On your way to boys' night? How 'bout the Crafty Beaver for a once-in-a-lifetime poke-'er match?"

What your average Jack won't dish out for a one-on-one! La Plata is all a guy's got for three hours in any direction—more, even, with Beantown all button-down-and-butt-plugged and Rudy done to Times Square what those transvestite hookers from Eighth Avenue used to do to him before he got that cherry bomb up his ass. The only other place that's any fun is the Mashpotato Indian Casino over the state line, and that's strictly stacked chance for truly strung-out gambling fiends. Unless you go to P-town, in which case you're a faggot. We've got our share of those places too here in La Plata.

"Step right up! Get your chin up in the sticky stuff!"

And for the buggerer on a budget, settling into a long, midlife marathon of compulsive pipe-cleaning, there's everyday-after-work visits to the bank of video booths at Arousing Superstore.

"A wanker is born every minute! Pick a flick! Pop it in! See what pops up!"

THE REST of it he laid out on a tabletop as velvet snortings for fiend days, with sniffers to match, while the other days of the week he snorted four figures in a snood of the vinyl soda straw.

MOUNT GOVERN, SATURDAY, 9:30 PM

THE flask is almost empty and the dust remaining on the mirror is barely enough to get my gums numb, so I decide to check in on a friend on Assmell Ave. Word in the Old World underworld is there's a new source in town. "Take me to Mount Govern, Sanchez. Stop at the bank so I can use the ATM."

The second my card starts to slip into the slot I notice a frost of white powder on the edge and I snap at the plastic. Too slow! The machine has swallowed and now the screen is asking for my password. I'm thinking *cancel!* What if the feds have got some kind of dust detectors built into these things and when you pop in your card and it's got traces on it an automatic signal goes to FBI headquarters and they see if you're anybody they want to finger? Fuck! Too late now. Two-eight-three-four. Withdrawal. Checking. Three-oh-oh enter. No to your fucking receipt. Two endless seconds go by and I know what the screen is going to say before it says it: *Busted.* Fuck you and your insufficient funds! I give the security camera the finger and go back to the car.

"Hey, Sanchez, they'll make a movie of me someday and you'll be a character, you know."

"Joo tink?"

"Joo bet. Remember the time we fucked up the guy who fucked my wife? That'll be a big scene. Who do you want to play you? Some spic hunk? Banderas, maybe?"

In the rearview, thick eyebrows flicker.

"Del Toro?"

Beady eyes widen.

"Leguizamo?"

"¿Leguizamo? ¡Carajo!"

"Okay, Leguizamo it is. Now be a pal, Sanchez, and lend me five bills."

"¡Ay, no! Again, jorona?"

"You know those paychecks you send your Tía Maria in Tijuana? Don't forget who signs them, kah-brone." Sanchez pulls out his clip.

Inside Mer de Tyranno, Franky Moccocco, the owner, greets me at the maitre d' station. "Hey, Pally!"

"Hey, Franky!"

"Pally, I'd like you to meet a frenamine. This is Dylan." *Frenamine* means he's okay, just like in *Donnie Brasco*. Unlike with *Donnie Brasco*, *frendaours* doesn't mean we're about to kill him, but it does mean watch what you say because he might be a narc.

"Hello, Dylan, I'm Pally Dimaio."

Dylan holds out a ghostly-white hand, cold to the touch. My friend Franky says, "Dylan is in da dry cleaning bidnis."

"I haven't heard of your business yet, have I, Dylan?" Dylan barely curls his upper lip. Franky ushers us through the kitchen to his back office and I hand Dylan three bills. "Start me off with an eight-ball. Don't give me any shit. You're going to sit here while I try it."

I'm already so zooted I don't know if I'll be able to tell the difference between Bogotá and baby aspirin, but I figure making him wait will guarantee he doesn't try to pass me three and a half grams of rat poison. Franky unhooks a small mirror from the wall and puts it on the desk. Dylan pulls out a fat little baggie about the size of the last joint of my thumb and pours the contents out on the glass. The pile is pure and luminous, bright as dry bleach. Dylan pulls out a stolen credit card. I catch a peek at the name embossed in green plastic: *"JIM FROST."* Chop chop chop. When he's got a couple of nice lines laid out, Dylan hands me a rolled-up twenty. *Snort! Snort!* It's good. Really good.

"I don't suppose I have to tell you, Dylan, that it wouldn't be nice to flap your gums to anyone about whose shirts you dry-clean."

"I'm a businessman," says Dylan. "What's good for business is good for me." Dylan takes back the twenty. I think he's going to stick it in his nose for a huff of his own but he just unrolls it and replaces it in his wallet.

"I thought that was my change."

He taps the little pile back inside the baggie and hands me the bindle. Bloodless, Dylan says, "Change?"

L IVING WITH him were a housekeeper in her for-
ties, a daughter who was not yet thirty, and a lad of
the shield-and-jackboot race who handled his car for
him and squealed on his screwy ex-wife.

POTENCY STREET, SATURDAY, 10:15 PM

"WAIT for me, Sanchez. I want to go out for a nightcap." When I get out of the car, Oprah opens the front door. "Hello, O, you fat-assed Jemima in a frilly apron."

Oprah sighs, "Po' Mizzes Mayo."

During the divorce, Shirley brainwashed the maid. Oprah is half-deaf and walks around talking to herself about what a scoundrel I am for abandoning poor, helpless Shirley—the bitch fleeced me for half a mil!—but I keep her around because she keeps an eye on my deadbeat daughter and babysits her bastard kid, plus she really knows how to cook up a mess of eggs.

I bought this place after the break-up and everybody said, "What are you, crazy? Shirley took the girl. You're a bachelor now. You should live in a condo." It's because I had to give Shirley five-hundred grand, and after that there was hardly anything left, but my friends don't get it: Real estate isn't real. Think you've got a million floating in mortgages? Not really. What's eight thousand bucks a month? Two grand a week? Two hundred and change a day? No more than a decent hotel. That's all you have to pay to surround yourself with luxury. And when you're ready to move, you sell at a profit, so over the years you drop maybe a couple of thou to live like a king, less than the blacks pay to rent in the projects and at the end of the road have nothing to show for it. This place is my divorce present to myself, my rebound pad, my palace. Cathedral ceilings, fireplaces in every room, Jacuzzi in the master bath. Plus the house is right around the corner from Antwerp's, a yuppie meat market with the choicest cunts.

I take off the toupee to give the cranium a breather, lay out a few lines on top of the glass coffee table, and settle in on the living room sofa for a little video.

Once upon a time a guy gets rid of his wife. Or she gets rid of him. It doesn't matter. He has girlfriends. She has boyfriends. The guy and his wife are sick of each other. The divorce is expensive and drags on a long time. The guy doesn't want her anymore but that doesn't stop him from feeling like throwing up when he finds out his old business partner is balling her. The guy thinks maybe he wants her back just to keep the prick from riding her ass, so he decides to try being nice to his wife. He brings her favorite dish to the house where they used to live together.

"When we get there, Sanchez, I want you to run up and ring the bell, and when she comes to the door, say real nice, 'This is from your old man.' You don't have to mention I'm in the car. She'll know." The divorce was final, but I knew she was going to appreciate this. Putanesca from Crapuloso. I was going to make a joke about how my *puta* days were over. I had a resolve. But when we got to the house I saw she wasn't alone. She had DiFelix, the prick, in there with her. He was getting ready to ride my wife's ass. It was like a mime act in a department-store window the way she touched his shoulder in front of the fireplace. There was smoke billowing out of the chimney. DiFelix had stoked a fire! That's what enraged me. DiFelix had stoked a fucking fire in my fucking fireplace (restraining order, sure; but I still paid the rent) and he was acting like he was going to fucking try and fuck my fucking wife. He *was* going to fucking try and fuck my fucking wife! "Sanchez, you thick spic, turn off the fucking headlights!"

"I dough like dis, jorona." Sanchez knew it stunk. He knew it was no good, sitting outside the house we were sitting outside of. "Wha I do wid de food?"

"Give it to your fucking dog."

"Wha eef he no Juan?"

"You got leather gloves, don't you? Shove it down his fucking throat. Where do they get you people for the academy these days?"

"Jorona, joo sure joo no Juan me drive joo home now?"

"No! You've got this shift 'til I'm finished for the night and you've got to stick with it, so shut the fuck up and collect your triple overtime, greaseball!" It lasted forever, the laying in wait. "You're not a cop, Sanchez. You know what you are? You're just a fucking donkey pulling a cart." Sweat beaded on the back of his neck. "Look at me when I talk to you! I'm sick of staring at the back of that hairy spic neck all fucking day!"

When they were finally finished fucking I followed DiFelix to make sure he went home and had Sanchez drive me back to my place, then I called the prick and invited him over for a little business meeting. Sanchez greeted DiFelix at the door and ushered him into my study. I had stoked a fire. DiFelix looked at me like he knew what was going to happen here. He did know what was going to happen here. Everybody knew. They just didn't know they knew. It was part of the fucking collective unconscious. They were waiting to know they knew. They were waiting until the rumor leaked and then a report showed up in the *La Plata Gazette* and then the charge got filed and the investigation began and the trial and testimony and *boom!* everyone knew they knew like they knew it all along, even all the stuff that didn't necessarily get said or done. "Really? The fireplace log?" "Yup. Had to piss on him to put him out!" "And the cop?" "Held the guy's arms for the cigarette treatment."

They talked about it over seven-dollar cocktails at Two Belfry Street and fifty-cent drafts at Boob's on the Shady Side. "Out on his *eyeball?*" Out on his eyeball. They talked about it.

I'm getting into the beginning of one of my favorite flicks when I hear the front doorbell ring and Oprah calls from the kitchen, "Y'all home, Mayo?"

"Hell no!"

"Daddy, it's me!" My daughter Leah bounces into the room. I zip up, don the wig, kick the paper to cover up the coke, and hit the remote, zapping *Troop Sex* into *La Plata*, a sappy show about a lady lawyer who can't or won't get laid. Should be called *Frigid in the City*. There goes my hard-earned hard-on!

"How are you, princess?"

Leah is sassy and sexy and looks a lot like her mother at twenty-one except with bigger tits. She lives with her little brat in an apartment nearby. "I need money, Pop." Cut to commercial: A gardener sprays the meanest weed-killer and a dandelion shrinks and shrivels in rapid time-lapse.

Catching my breath, I adjust the toupee. "You ought to go on public assistance, Leah. You're old enough, you know."

Leah loves her dad. Here's how she shows it: She plops down in my lap, puts her arms around my neck, and simpers, "You know I'm daddy's widdle *grrrl*."

I hand Leah a hundred. "You're turning out just like your whore of a mother, Leah."

"She's the whore you married, Daddy."

"Most expensive whore I never fucked."

"Can't Daddy gimme a widdle *mooor?*" I fork over my last hundred and Leah gets up. I slap her ass and she scampers off to the kitchen where Oprah is cooking something for her to soak up a little of whatever Leah does to get high on a Saturday night in La Plata.

THIS 'GINA man of ours was close on to fifty, of a rotund constitution and with no little flesh on his bones and a face that was fat and droopy. He was noted for his late carousing, being very fond of the cunt.

SOUTH MEAN STREET, SATURDAY, 10:45 PM

I GO back outside to the car. "Antwerp's, Sanchez." No time for lines. I tap two little piles of powder onto the back of my hand and snuff them up. Sanchez opens the door and I check the mirror and climb out. The bar is packed, but you goddamn better believe they saved me my table in back. The owner has been very accommodating since a new waiter tried handing me a tab last month and as a result the fire marshal started making unannounced visits.

A nightcap turns into four or five snifters of cognac, a steak, and a couple of appetizer platters for some friends who stop by my table. Around closing time I have the bartender refill my flask with B&D and I stumble out to the car.

THEY WILL try to tell you his surname was Domino or D'amato—there is some difference of opinion among those who have written on the subject—but according to the most likely conjectures we are to understand that it was really Dimaio. But all this means very little so far as our story is concerned, providing that in the telling of it we do not depart one iota from the truth.

WONCHASUCKIT RIVER, SUNDAY, 2:30 AM

SANCHEZ, pull over so I can piss in the river."
"Why no joo go een de resaran, jorona?"
"Why do you give a shit where I pee, Pancho? You
want to unzip me too? Pull over at the goddamn river, you
limp-dick spic!"

Sanchez pulls up to the curb near the mouth of the
Wonchasuckit. I climb out of the car and stagger to the rail
where the river spills into the bay. Hooking the neck of the flask
with one finger, I fumble with my fly and whip out Rock
Sinatra. He hits the air streaming and my piss splits the river
with a splat-sizzle. Steam rises from the surface.

I thought maybe I could shut DiFelix up, not by bribing him
but by demanding a bribe not to kill him. "You're fucking my
wife. You're going to give me a hundred-thousand bucks."
DiFelix pressed charges anyway. There was an investigation and
naturally I left some dents in his flesh. I pleaded no contest,
gave up the office, and got a suspended sentence. In some ways
I'm glad for what happened with DiFelix and my wife. Bottom
line is I was in my prime: thirty-nine (for the fourth or fifth
time), single again, a couple of reliable connections to coke, not
to mention a few close doctor friends, which means a steady
supply of Valiums and other yums. There were three things I
wanted. I wanted to be drunk, I wanted to be fucking a lot of

hot women, and I wanted to be snorting a ton of cocaine. Where better to do all of the above than at any of the several gentlemen's clubs run by some of my highest campaign contributors? Drinks were free, naturally, and so was snatch. Coke came with the ho's. By day I did the radio thing, gassing on about whatever was on people's minds, while by night I made the most of my time out of the spotlight. For five years, all I did was eat, drink, and fuck for free, then sleep, wake up, and coke up in time for the afternoon talk show. Broadcast was pretty much the same idea as politics: braggery and bullying. But it wasn't as much fun sitting in a studio as putting my body into it all over the city. I missed being mayor. As soon as the statute against felons running for office was up, I was back in the race. My campaign slogan: *"I'm gonna make love to La Plata again!"*

The fog here doesn't drop or roll in. It emerges from the water, a thick mist with a low-down tidal whiff. It's a fishy dip, all right, the kind that creeps right up on the continental lip after a long, lurching journey straight from the black depths, the Odor Out of Time old boys like William Rogers and Abraham Beige smelled on this very road back when it was cobblestone. I glance over my shoulder. Sanchez has left the park lights on, but those yellow splotches are blotted out as I watch. The banks in my little cityscape compose a skyline that from two hundred yards you can fit in a fist. One by one their lights are extinguished, first the flickering lantern atop venerable old Armada Bank, then the crown of patriotic lamps around Monarch's head. Finally, the only things left shining are the three beaming boobs at the corners of Proletarian Trust.

"Sanchez?" No answer. Standing there raising the level of the Wonchasuckit a few inches—I must have drunk a barrel of B&D!—I take a long pull from the flask. A whiff of fish interrupts my piss, stemming the stream. That little switch that keeps piss from getting mixed up with jiz goes *flick!* That's what happens when I get a sniff of fish. The vapor in the air makes my nose tingle, activating crystals caked deep in my nostrils, and those tits on top of Proletarian Bank start reduplicating. Boobs are bouncing all over the sky while I ride Rock Sinatra.

YOU MAY know, then, that the aforesaid 'gina man, on those occasions when he was at leisure, which was most of the night around, was in the habit of viewing flicks of ribaldry with such pleasure and devotion it led him almost wholly to forget the life of a mayor and even the administration of his estate. So great was his curiosity and infatuation in this regard that he even skipped many payments of alimony in order to be able to rent and view as many of the flicks that he loved, and he would carry home with him as many of them as he could on tape.

Of all the flicks that he thus devoured, none pleased him so well as the ones that had been performed by the famous Dolly Dellabutta, whose juicy pose style and revolving seat were as luscious to him as pearls; especially when he came to beat those tails of love and amorous phalanges that are to be met with in many places, such asses of the boweling, for example: *"The creaming of the reaming that affects my rear, in such a manner weakens my reaming that I with creaming laminate your cumliness."* And he was similarly infected when his thighs fell upon such asses as these: *". . . the high heaving of your rigidity rigidly fortifies you with the ass and renders you perverting of that pervert your greatness doth perve."*

POTENCY STREET, SUNDAY, 3:00 AM

LEAH has picked up the kid and Oprah has gone home. It's now, in the middle of the night, when there's nobody to call, nothing to busy myself with, that I wouldn't mind having a wife. Someone to rub against. Someone in the morning to take care of the breakfast and dry cleaning, make sure there's no stains on my jacket. This is when I almost miss married life and I know I'm some kind of lonely troll living in a tree all alone.

For five terrific years between my first and second terms, it was a-stripper-a-day-keeps-the-cocktease-away, but something happened to me around the time I started running for mayor again. I had just turned forty (five times over) and the five-year fantasy was finished. I discovered I couldn't get lead with a regular lady around anymore. She could be a slut I take out to eat every now and then or the kind of whore paid for in cash, but either way Rock Sinatra was a flop. Callgirls and girlfriends worked ol' Rock with the loosest larynxes. Some tried stuffing him right up in the clam, but Sinatra wouldn't firm up or spit up until he and I were all alone. The little blue pill just left us blue-balled. It got Rock stiff but it was more like rigor mortis than a hard-on. It was no picnic. It hurt. I wanted to get off, but no chance.

A friend of mine who owns Arousing Superstore brought

me a thick brown envelope. "For your return to the public eye," he said.

"Jesus, Joe! Give it to Hank. You know to bring all thank-yous to Cantare!"

"Don't worry, Pally. It's not that kind of donation. Take a look."

Inside the envelope was a porn video. "What the fuck?"

"Check it out. The first Dolly Dellabutta. If you like it, I've got more. She churns out a new one every week."

At first I was like, *Fuck this, Donald Dimaio does not do stroke flicks,* but when I popped it in the VCR it didn't take long for me to get hooked on that ass. *That ass that ass that ass.* Dolly is a butt-man's fantasy and the reverse-angle camera is a main feature of her movies. Half the actors ball her in her opera box. With most porn it takes me long and vigorous manipulation to achieve even a chubber, but Dellabutta's flicks are another story. Now Dolly, shot from behind, is the only way to get Rock hard. When a tits-and-ass woman's around I'm out of service, but alone with my Dolly Dellabutta collection I can break the sperm bank.

I'm wired and the house is goddamn quiet. Not just no-traffic-outside quiet, but there's-nothing-else-living-inside-this-brick-box quiet. I'm in bed in my mansion, alone with the video harem, when tits turn into stiff pricks.

THE POOR fellow used to lie awake nights in an effort to dingle-dangle the reaming and make sex out of asses such as these, although Casanova himself would not have been able to underhand them, even if he had been red-erected for that hole, purse-posed. He was not at ease in his hind over those wands that Long Dong gave and relieved; for no matter how great the virgins who treated him, the poor fellow must have been left with their fascia and their entire booty covered with marks and scars. Nevertheless, he was grateful to the flogger for coozing the flick with the promise of an internal indenture to come; many a time he was tempted to take up his penis and literally finish the tail as had been prodded, and he redoubtably would have done so, and would have sucked seed very well, if his tauts had not been constantly occupied with other slings of greater tomentum.

POTENCY STREET, SUNDAY, 10:00 AM

I WAKE up with an animal appetite and want some eggs but Oprah is nowhere to be found. I put on my robe and open the front door. "Where'd you go, O? Out to straddle the old Sambo lamppost?" No mail in the box and the Sunday *La Plata Gazette* on the step. Oh yeah, it's Oprah's day off.

Cantare shows up, surgical tape on his face and a box of donuts under his arm.

"Nice touch for your wedding day, Hank. Good luck convincing your guests it wasn't the bride."

"I won't even try. I figure she's my best alibi. Did you read the editorial yet?"

I turn to the opinions page and see the headline: "*Corruption at City Hall? Business As Usual.*"

"That fuckface Sukoff! When I take over the *PlaGa* I'm going to have that prick publisher bring me coffee in his gartered, bare butt!"

Cantare drops the box on the kitchen table and flips up the top. Nestled among the nuts and crullers is a thick-stuffed envelope. "From a friend at the tow association."

"Which one?"

"Ricky Zitirello."

"How much?"

"Three Gs."

"All right. Keep Three Zs on the list."

Three Zs is Ricky Zitirello's garage. All the shop owners in La Plata know the golden rule Police Captain Umberto Umbilico teaches his cadets from day one: If it moves, ticket it; if it don't, tow it. Towing is a ten-million-a-year business in this city. You got a garage and want your trucks to be on the call list? First you pay Cantare your annual fee. Never less than five grand. Ten if you want to stay in good graces. Cantare keeps his delivery fee and the rest goes to a good cause: me.

I take the eight-ball and throw it on the table for Cantare to chop us a few breakfast toots. "Get to work."

"Hey! Pretty quick on the rebound, boss!" He pours out a little pile and starts drawing lines.

"Sit down, why don't you, Hank?"

"Can't. Goddamn tetanus shot."

While we take turns over the glass tabletop, Cantare tries to convince me of what a great girl he's about to shackle up with.

"Wait'll you get a load of Stella, boss. Tits, ass, and sass! I knew I had to marry her from the first fuck."

"You can have it. I'm happier being a bachelor. I've got this one girl Dolly who's got a tail like a Chevy. She lets me ride it whenever I want, and when I'm done she doesn't need any of that goddman attention. No 'take me out' or 'talk to me' or anything. It's just fuck and sleep."

"Sounds pretty good. Maybe you should make her your full-time old lady."

"No way, Hank. Fucking the same whore every night gets so fucking monotonous. Do you have any idea how much free pussy I get as mayor? Marriage, on the other hand . . ."

"Oh, no." Cantare has heard this rap.

"It's like the chefs put a banquet with food from every part of the world in front of you, but day after day after day you can only eat the same thing."

"Eggs," Cantare says.

"Eggs. Other guys get Italian, Chinese, Spanish, French, Caribbean. You smell how good it all is. You're licking your lips. You want to try a little of everything yourself, but you're always forced to pick the same dish. Eggs. You try them prepared different styles for a while and sauce it up a little every now and then—Benedict one day, ranchero the next—but after a time even that goes dry and all that's left is scrambled and it's not even fresh: *powdered* eggs."

"I know, boss, I know."

"It's not over yet. One day you show up for the smorgasbord and where your platter of eggs used to be there's something floating in a glass jar full of murky brine like some kind of abortion. You're like, 'Where's my eggs?' And the waiter says, 'In there.' Now it's *pickled* eggs. For the rest of your goddamn life. You're hungry as hell and they've still got all that good stuff laid out to either side. Tortellini, roast duck, beef with broccoli."

"I hear you, boss."

"You sit and watch while all around you other guys are dipping their fingers straight in the gravy or diving right into dessert—chocolate-chip blondies à la mode! oh!—but all you get is eggs. Pickled eggs. That's what it's like having a wife."

"Only my Stella's not eggs, Pally. Stella is like . . . she's like . . . sushi!"

"Sushi? Uncooked fish?"

"Yeah! Rice and vegies too. All the food groups, nutritionally complete. You could eat it every night."

"Maybe a Jap." I snuff up the last of my five lines. "Not me."

IN SHORT, our 'gina man became so perverse in his viewings that he spent whole nights from sundown to sunup and his days from dawn to dusk in pouring over his flicks, until, finally, from so little sleeping and so much beating, his vein dried up and he went completely out of his mind.

MACNAMARA PLAZA, SUNDAY, 1:15 PM

SANCHEZ swings by to pick me up for breakfast. Quiche at Inferno, where my table is always waiting. After my cognac I head to City Hall and duck in the private entrance to my office, heading straight for the mahogany bar bought on campaign funds to entertain visiting ding-dongs. I pour myself a glass from my bottle of press-conference water (vodka over rocks), settle into the big leather chair, and press the button on the intercom. "Dotty?"

"Good afternoon, Mayor."

Good old Dot, the perfect executive assistant: always at her desk, doesn't know what Sunday is, doesn't have a life. Too bad she's a wrinkled old dog, but if Dotty was sexy she'd also be stupid and I'd never get any work done. Fortunately, most days I don't even have to look at her thanks to the intercom.

"What we got?"

"Members luncheon at the Cap 'n' Gown."

"Tell those fuckers to fuck off."

"I'll send them your regrets. Then there's Mr. Cantare's wedding reception."

"Get me something ready for that."

"I'll leave an envelope with Sanchez. By the way, Mayor, today's your sister's anniversary."

"What'd I get her?"

"A scarf, a necklace, and some earrings."

"How much?"

"Two hundred on her and three hundred on your brother-in-law for infrared golf binoculars."

"Take it out of the campaign. Anything else?"

"Just your one o'clock meeting, Mayor."

"One o'clock? What the fuck?"

"Tommy Fritos."

"Who the fuck scheduled this?"

"He said Mr. Cantare asked him to set it up."

"Fuck Mr. Cantare! Hank knows I don't do Sunday meetings. Cancel it!"

"Mr. Fritos is out in the hall, Mayor."

"Tell him I'm not here. I'll go out my private door."

"He was just commenting to me how Officer Sanchez almost knocked him down when he opened your door a minute ago."

"Motherfucker!" I'm considering bolting out the back when I remember what I've got in my desk. "All right, Dotty. Wait five minutes, then send the asshole in."

"Yes, Mayor."

Right-side drawer, underneath the note cards with the seal of the city, inside the Bible, carved out of Corinthians, there's a compact mirror with four lines already laid out where I left them yesterday afternoon. Pinch left, right, left, right. *Fsst! fsst! fsst! fssst!* I put the Bible away and there's a knock at the door. "Come in!" *you little shit.* Fritos enters the second I'm hit between the eyes by the icy spike.

"Goo moaning, Mayor. I love you spich last night."

"What can I do for you, Tommy?"

"Nuthin', Mayor. I wondering what I do for you."

"Oh yeah?"

"Sure. Brautway grow so much this year I wanna put a little back inda city."

"Ha! You already do, Tommy. It's built-in, in fact. Or don't you pay your business tax?"

"Evy munt. But I thought I maybe put it somewhere else. Maybe right in you funraise."

I don't like the sound of this. Fritos is speaking the right language but it's coming out all wrong. Too cocky. Too cool. I level crosshairs on him. "Is that all you came in to talk about?"

"I bring you a connibyooshun."

"You know you're supposed to take this stuff up with Hank."

"I know, I know. I just wonder if you want a connibyooshun straight from me sometime." Sneaky Portaguee opens his coat and pulls out an envelope right there.

There's something I've known as far back as I can remember: There are people who are friends and there are people who are not. A great arc like a stormfront on the weather chart envelops the loyal ones, while outside the curve we quarantine the disloyal: the ones who don't give and take, the ones who question and talk, and the ones who—a word that, even with its barnyard associations, doesn't begin to approximate the despicable nature of their behavior—squeal.

"No thanks, Tommy. Put that thing away." I stand up so Fritos knows it's time to go and he puts the envelope back in his pocket. He passes me one of those gross stogies instead.

"Okay, Mayor, but lemme remind you I put inna low bid onna schools department lease. My building's good building. Just what they ask for inna RFP."

"I'll try to see that you get a good rating, Tommy." I let that hang in the air and walk Fritos to the door. I don't have to complete the instructions by naming the condition: Pay Hank, *pagare Cantare*. It's understood in any lingo.

La Plata is a town on the take. You want to be a cop? Five will get you into the academy. If my mother knew your mother, maybe three. You got tax problems? I'll have the examiner fix it. A hundred-thousand in back payments magically becomes ten for a friend, twenty if you're a regular guy, and even if you're just a prick Jew we can probably pull it down to fifty. Whatever kind of business you do there's always tickets for campaign events. Or, as mush-mouth Tommy Fritos puts it: funraise. One-twenty-five five times a year. Or if you own a shop of some kind, a yard and a quarter for ten. Every time a Pals of Pally dinner comes around Hank stops by and hands you a booklet. You say, "I don't know what to do with all these." He says, "Take 'em. I don't care what you do with 'em. Sell 'em to your mechanics. Give 'em away to your friends. Light your cigars with 'em. But give me fucking twelve-fifty." Money is respect, the purest form. Everyone could be happy if they'd just look at money for what it is, a token of loyalty. It's not so much that money is required to play. More like the absence of money is an insult. Someone who doesn't realize this doesn't even deserve a setting-straight. Just let him go away. So pay up on time and don't get on our bad side. It could cost you a lot more.

Take the Cap 'n' Gown Club, wedged between the La Plata School of Technical Crafts and Beige University, though this ivory-league rip-off society doesn't have anything to do with either. It's just a bunch of cravat-and-spats fags who like to prance around and pretend they never let go of their good ol' fraternity days. Chug a brew or two, sing "Boola Boola," circle-jerk on a chocolate-chip cookie—*Last one eats it!* Lunches suck and even state reps have to pay the check, something any respectable politician shouldn't do in this town. I fucked them over and took the membership but I don't ever go there. I can eat a much classier meal for free across the river at Crapuloso. But you don't go to Cap 'n' Gown Club for the food. You can run the city forever and miss out on a piece of some of the biggest contracts if every now and then you don't rub shoulders with the Beige brothers and the great-great-grandson of William Rogers and a hundred-something inbred heirs of the original pilgrims. Certain deals can be brokered only in their Mayflowery mist. But the main reason I applied is I knew there were some old blue-blood fuckers trying to keep me out. They didn't want any names that end in vowels on their roll. Whenever I called, the membership director milked mine for four or more syllables. "No decision yet on your application, Mr. Dim-ay-i-o." Made me sound like chicken-fucking Old McDonald! They thought they could shit on me. Behind closed doors they called me guido. They called me wop and I-ti. They called me dago and Guinea. The stupider Aryans couldn't even discriminate properly and called me nigger or spic. Fuck 'em. Nobody keeps me out of the club. I sent inspectors to slap violations all over their lily-white asses. They lost building permits like I did hair in my thirties. If they wanted more than a gravel lot to dine on I was going to make them swallow every last one of those epithets. The membership director ate "spic" on a stick. The Beige brothers nibbled "nigger" like spray cheese on endive. Billy Rogers III slurped cold "I-ti" on the half shell, swished it around with some sauvignon blanc, and gulped it whole. It didn't take long to starve them out. In a few weeks I got my apology and a free lifetime membership. The hand you slam the door on today is connected to the dick you lick tomorrow.

Being mayor is kind of like one big wedding party. I'm the groom and La Plata is my wife. Welcome to my wedding! You're invited to kiss the bride, but don't forget the time-honored tradition of stuffing the sack. I'll take you right up her inner thigh, but you better be ready to stick the envelope in or it's out on your ass in the Rawbucket River. I'm the groom and the city is my wife. Or I'm the motherfucking bride and Cantare is the sack. Either way, she's holding it open to you. Well? What are you going to do? That's right, money in an envelope: Here comes the bribe, all dressed in white!

With Fritos out of the way I decide it's time for a change. I go over to the bar and press the button to open the secret compartment. What's it going to be today? The Flattop? Nah. Too tame. The Brushcut? Better save it for the parade. I haven't worn the Pachuco since I got saddled with Sanchez. How about the Boogie? The Butch? The Ducktail, a.k.a. DA?

All those natural bastards grandmaternally gifted with a great tuft on top never stop and think about the hard choices a guy like me has to make every day. The fundamental difference between their fleece and my piece: Real hair is alive and responds to its environment like petals on a stem. With me it's like an artificial plant. I've got to be on top of the day's perils and possibilities or my mane will look woefully out of place. There's nothing more damaging to a political image than arriving at an eight-alarm fire wearing a slick codfish like you just showed up for a supermarket grand opening.

Here's the one I call the Jesus, not so much longer but a little shaggier than the rest, strictly for first communions. When I stride up to the front pew, all those meaty Italian mothers, moist under their best dresses, pick up subliminally what was on Christ's mind same as mine: *Eat me.* This one, John the Baptist, bristly like on a guy who's just had the surprise of his life, I reserve mostly for christenings. At funerals I wear the Peter, a monkish down that in the mellow light of the mortuary creates a slight halo effect, which, in combination with the prescriptionless smart-guy glasses I use for art openings and theater premiers, gives me the grave, contemplative aura of a saint standing over the casket and trying to decide whether to admit the deceased through the pearly gates. I usually let the poor fucker in, unless he owes me money.

Today's a wedding day, so I remove my morning Fuzzcut and put on the Cupid with its cherubic wisps. The Cupid makes me look cute, and wedding receptions are where I used to get the best flying fucks. The bride-groom-aisle spectacle causes your overripe thirty-something bird to freak out. She worries she's never going to find Mr. Right, some live-in drunk to beat her up for the rest of her life, so she drowns her warts in champagne and an extra slice of three-tier cake and submits to a slow, standing screw inside a banquet hall broom closet. I swear, just the memory of it is enough to sustain me through the gag-amateur toasts and all that maddening polka music.

HE HAD filled his imagination with every sling that he had viewed, with enhancements, nightly end-chowders, bottles, phalanges, wands, with tails of love and tits' torrents, and all sorts of imp-awful slings, and as a result had come to relieve that all these dick-lick-us strappings were chewed; they were more rear to him than any sling-elf in the hurl.

CRAMPTON, SUNDAY, 4:20 PM

SANCHEZ drops me off at the entrance to Two Elms. People are already drunk and dirty. There has been booze, plenty of it, beginning before the ceremony. There's so much free liquor in my profession it's sick. At Italian weddings I'm supposed to get good and drunk. It would be an insult to the father of the bride if I didn't. Parents seriously believe I'll bring the marriage good luck when I arrive. I show up and suddenly all the guests know they're in the right place. Let's have another drink! Even the ones who minutes ago were thinking, *God, what an awful party!* are suddenly all, *The Mayor's here! What a blowout!*

You can hardly hear yourself speak over the accordion player's hysterics. In the receiving line, I shout at the father, "You must feel like a very lucky man!"

"I have a toss at Sodom, I've chained a bun."

"Pardon?"

"I haven't lost a daughter, I've gained a son."

"Oh, yeah, congratulations."

"Hello," the mother moos. She's big, nylons bulging. Lines pushing through the sheer fabric of her dress show a barrel-shaped butt puckering out of parachute bloomers.

"The bride sure cried, ma'am. How 'bout you?"

"I'm twice as reary and a lot fatter."

"What was that?"

"I'm twice as teary and a lot sadder."

"Well, uh, congrats." I've got to move on. I must be pretty fucked-up. I spot Cantare with the bandage on his face at the bar. "Hey, Hank!" I reach with the right. "Happy ball-and-chain!"

"Thanks, boss!" I cover our shake with my left hand and crush Cantare's hand, drilling my law school class ring into his knuckle. "Ouch!"

I pull Cantare close and press mouth to ear. I'm licking my teeth and gnawing on my lower lip. "What the fuck were you thinking sending Fritos straight to me?"

"What are you talking about, Pally?"

"And on a Sunday, goddamnit!"

"But boss—"

"But *fuck.* He tried to pass me a thank-you right in my fucking office. He's got his briefcase, Virgin Mary cufflinks, a tiepin with the Portaguee flag, and a half-dozen more places to hide a camera or wire. What are the fucking odds he *wasn't* trying to fuck me?"

"I swear, Pally—"

"Swear all you want on your dead mother's hairy ass. From now on, nothing ever comes to me except through you, *capisce?* I don't care if it's my fucking granddaughter who wants to give me her piggy bank. Nobody ever connects a payment straight to me." A couple of drunk cops come over to buffet Cantare with backslaps so I decide to drop it. Hank got the message. I let go of his hand and go for the wife.

Stella isn't young. She doesn't have big tits. She's not even particularly beautiful. But she wears tight, nude-colored stockings under an ass-hugging mini-gown, and she's got a crooked grin that reminds me of my favorite porn star. "Hello, Mrs. Cantare." Of course she knows who I am when I walk over and pucker up. "I'm here to collect."

Stella plants a sweet, sticky kiss on my lips. "Me too," she says, holding her sack open to me. My left hand slips in a business envelope full of fifties. No name on the front, but they'll know who it came from. The envelope is embossed with the seal of the city. I reach around with my right hand and pull Stella close. Her mom was wrong: Stella is nearly as big in the rear.

"You know your new husband works for me, but sometimes he makes me wonder whether it's really the other way around. You might feel that way too, but always remember who's really boss."

"Oh, I don't claim to wear the pants," says Stella. She's got this sleepy, squeezed expression that makes her look kind of doped-up and Chinese. Dunaway-in-*Chinatown* Chinese. "But when he gets home I make sure he keeps them down around his ankles."

I go out to the car to snort some coke. Stella makes me think. I say to myself, 'Keeps them down around his ankles!' She says this to me one-on-one, with Cantare just out of earshot. What are the chances she wants to fuck me?

HE WOULD remark that Marilyn Chambers had been a very good night erotic, but there was no comparison between her and Debbie Does Dallas, who with a single backward choke had cut in half two fierce and monstrous 'ginas.

DONNY DOES COLONICS

KING Lorne lives in Wichita, a vast empire with every species you can imagine, all of the animals hunting and mating (whatever that means) under a fiery sun embossed with the feather-dressed profile of an Indian chief. This much I can make out between all the big words and dazzling pictures. It's the world's wildest zoo without the cages, and I visit one night a week. I can't wait for dark and each next episode. I don't know what to do with my afternoons.

Mama asks why I'm so forlorn. "I want us to move to Kansas." When I tell her it's because of Liason of Wichita's *Untame Domain*, she smiles and sets me up in my father's office with a stack of magazines. The photographs are terrific, all my favorites: cheetahs, elephants, giraffes, water buffalo. They must have been shot in Wichita. After I've flipped through the entire stack I pick another magazine off my father's shelf, open it, and find the place where the pages lay flat. That means someone looks at this spread a lot, where there's a picture of a different kind of animal. In my father's leather chair, by the dim yellow light coming through the pulled shade, that's where it first surprises me: the stiffness. I think something must be wrong with me. The only time I've experienced swelling like this has been after falling off my bike, and that was my foot, not my weenie. What hit me? I don't make the connection with the pictures.

My dad comes in and sees me in his leather chair. "What

the hell are you doing in here?" He spots the journal spread open on the desk. The corners of his mouth curl down and his eyes dart to the empty spot on the shelf. He looks back at me and his upper lip wiggles. It's ugly, that face. It's like the hyena's on *Untame Domain*. What did the announcer say that expression is supposed to mean? Fear? Arousal? A combination? Liason of Wichita is into combinations. The red flush on my father's bald head is like when he drinks wine and listens to records late at night. I turn red too. At least I feel like I do. My cheeks are burning. My father marches over and flips the magazine closed. I'm looking down at the desk and the embossed lettering on the cover. Although it's much longer than my three- and four-letter specialties, the word looks familiar because I've seen it written a bunch of times after my father's last name, which is my last name, and I've heard it pronounced with words whose parts sound pretty much the same. "Practice," "doctor," "apology." My father's huge, nimble hand rests on the gray dust jacket. There's the silver ring that says he went to school to be a doctor, right alongside the gold band that says he married my mother. He slowly slides the magazine out of sight of my downturned eyes. Do I know what's coming or do I just think *I knew it was coming* a second after it happens? It's so fast—*whack!*—not the soft leather of his open hand but the embossed cardboard of the magazine cover. It brands the side of my face with the word "*Proctology*."

It's in one of my father's medical journals that I get my first look at a woman's ass. Then again, who knows? In extreme close-up, it could have been a man's. Either way, the ass was diseased. From then on, the doctor's office is kept locked.

H E PREFERRED Harry Reems, who in *Deep Throat* had played the Doc, despite the smarm the latter bore, availing himself of the microscope which he coolly employed when he examined Linda Lovelace, the clit in the back of her throat.

CHANNEL 8, SUNDAY, 6:00 PM

*L**INDA:*** "A white-cheeked gibbon is on the loose after escaping from William Rogers Park zoo during a routine feeding late last night."

Harry [stock footage: monkeys]: "Monkeys have tails. Apes do not. Gibbons have no tails, so they are not monkeys at all. They are apes."

Linda [stock footage: mayor cutting ribbon]: "Mayor Donald 'Pally' Dimaio opened the new William Rogers Park zoo with a ribbon-cutting ceremony during his first administration. Two hundred thousand people visit there every year and so far there have been no escapes."

Harry [repeat stock footage: monkeys]: "While this gibbon is not considered particularly dangerous, apes can carry diseases such as rabies and tetanus in their saliva, and citizens of La Plata are warned to keep pets inside and windows and doors closed. If you see the gibbon in your neighborhood, keep away and call the police, whose veterinary professionals will return the gibbon to the zoo for his own health and protection. Say, Tony, what's the weather going to be like for that gibbon tonight?"

Tony [cut to: meteorologist]: "Well, Harry. Gibbons are native to the Asian *rain*forests, and it looks like we'll be able to give him some of that in the forecast for tomorrow. Heh heh."

H E HAD much good to say for Emanuelle, who, though she belonged to the haughty, overbearing race of 'ginas, was of a stackable position and well bra'd up.

EDEN STREET, SUNDAY, 9:00 PM

CRUISING down Adamo Avenue we blow by Arousing Superstore and I start telling Sanchez some more about the girlfriend he's never met. "Dolly turns it on whenever I want. Where other sluts let up, she always carries on, and when I'm finished, she doesn't bitch about an orgasm. Dolly presses her own button. Sometimes I like to sit back and watch." We're almost at the Arrow Street bridge when I realize I'm on my last smoke. "Oh, Pancho?" I say lovingly, like his fucking father.

"Jes, jorona?"

I lean over the frontseat and exhale a cloud of mentholated smoke in his face. "Pull over at the gas station and get me some fucking cigarettes, you lard-ass spic." Some dogs are happier on a short leash. This is one of them.

Sanchez parks near the pumps at the Eden Street Sesh station and leaves the engine running. I'm watching him cut to the front of the line and push a bill in the cashier's trap door when all of a sudden there's a sharp tap at the glass. Outside the back window something dark spins into my periphery. A pistol! I duck and ball myself up on the floor between the seats, but I know it won't do any good. Whoever it is—a Matriarcha-made man or a fanatical feminist—has finally caught up with me and brought a big enough gun so the bullet-proof glass won't make a difference. Time's up. Here comes the slug. Dear Jesus, please forgive me for all that dirty stuff!

Nothing happens.

I peek and there's the pistol, still spinning in the tinted air, but turns out it's just a gas nozzle. What the fuck? The fuel line wiggles up in the window like the charmed snake in Ali Baba. I push the button to lower the glass, peer outside, and see the hairy fist.

"*Ook ook! Ai ai ai!*"

The white-cheeked gibbon twirls the gas line like a swinging vine and catches the nozzle in his other paw. He rolls back the plastic hood, the part that's supposed to lower emissions, and squeezes the trigger, squirting a stream of 87 octane, the cheap shit, smack in the middle of my lap. The gasoline soaks through the wool pants and the vapors start to burn. In reflex I brush the spill with the back of my hand but I'm still pinching the butt end of my last cigarette and I accidentally tap red ash. The pants light up. I fling open the door, knocking the nozzle out of the escaped ape's hands and sending the little fucker tumbling. I lunge for the windshield cleaner, upending the suspended bucket and splashing sudsy liquid on my crotch just in time to save my balls from burning off. I kneel wheezing on the asphalt by the side of the sedan. My pants are sopping wet and reek of blue fluid. Sinatra is singed and freezing but the fire is out.

Sanchez comes back to the car with my carton of smokes. "Jorona! Wha'pen?"

"You fat fuckface! Catch that little shit!"

"What leetle sheet?"

"The goddamn gibbon!"

Sanchez spends half an hour searching the station and surrounding blocks, but the fugitive has disappeared into the night. "I swear it was that fucking ape. He was laughing like a fucking hyena."

Or maybe it's like a gibbon he was laughing.

B UT, ABOVE all, he cherished an admiration for Long Dong Silver, especially as he beheld him sallying forth from his asshole to rub all those that crossed his path, or when he thought of him overseas peeling the phalange of *Sex Freaks* which, so the story has it, was below his knees.

YOUNG DON SNIVELER

IN catechism class, Sister Marie Aloysius, flashing her half-
toothless grin at me, rants, "Young man, either you believe
in God, or you've got to believe you *are* God." That
checkerboard smile is challenging me. *Make God, boy,* it says. *Be
God.* It's around this time that the question is posed to me:
"What do you want to do when you grow up?" My first thought
is I want to be on television, but not like Eisenhower or
Cronkite. I want to be Durante.

The thought of my father's closed, locked office haunts me
throughout my childhood. To distract myself I watch more TV.
You can depend on television. You're not going to see a picture
of someone's blistering anus, for instance, wedged between
Liason of Wichita's *Untame Domain* and an ad for Mick's
Mentho-rub. There's a local kiddy show called *Child's Play.* My
mother telephones the lady producer, a friend of hers, and
makes an appointment for the woman to be my voice coach. In
a few weeks I'm on TV wearing oversized overalls smudged
with stage mud and a little wax moustache on my upper lip,
singing, *"Where do ya worka, John?"* Around the set of *Child's
Play* they call me their Everything Boy.

In the middle of the season I catch a chest cold that keeps
me off the show for two straight weeks. My father brings me a
little brown bottle. "I probably shouldn't be giving this to you,
but it's the best remedy there is."

Codeine. I start with a measured teaspoon like the label says, but before long I'm pouring a lazy capful, then swigging a teaspoon or four straight from the bottle. Every six hours turns into every coupla hours turns into *what the fuck is a clock?* I understand I'm onto something special. I start to fake coughing fits. I sneak my mother's smokes to give myself yellow phlegm.

One day, home "sick" from school on a cruise as Kid Codeine, I'm curled up with some pillows and my bottle on the living room couch, where my mother has set me up in front of the TV at the edge of oblivion. I swoon in an opiate surge and find my hand pinned between my hip and the back of the couch. I can't feel my fingers and I can't move the arm. The whole shebang has fallen asleep. I figure I'll pry the pinned hand out from under me with my other arm, but that won't move either. I'm paralyzed. I can't move anything at all. My eyes are open, my chin against my chest, and I can see down the length of my prone body, but nothing will budge. Maybe I'm dead. I've heard about overdoses. This must be how it happens. Have I already been embalmed? I lie there unable to move, speak, or cry. Finally, after ten seconds that feel like forever, a tingle comes to my fingers, and by a mammoth concentration I make the fingertips wiggle. My hand gives a weak squeeze, the arm aches back to life, and I stiffly rise from the couch.

A few years later in prep school at Abraham Beige Academy I first try cocaine. Some kid's dad is addicted and one day he just leaves a pile out on the kitchen table, so we stick our faces in it and start huffing. Nicholas Capellini, the kid whose house it is, fritzes out on the spot and ends up with some kind of nerve damage. They have to take him off the wrestling team. Me, I feel nothing unusual. Just the back of my throat goes a little itcy-numb like at the dentist.

Twenty-five years go by before I try it again, at a bachelor party for a buddy. He presses a miniature baggie into my palm. "What is this?" I say. "I don't want this. I'm going into politics."

"Trust me, you want this."

"I don't want this!"

"Pally, you want this."

I try it. He's right. I want it. Before long barely a week goes by without a noseful. After a few months it's more like never a day. For a while I try to keep the noon rule: no coke in the morning. Of course, it doesn't count as morning if I stay up all night. When three grams takes me straight through to 6:30 AM, then the twentieth line before passing out at sunrise is still the last line of the night. Then one Monday when I'm already mayor, Sanchez is waiting out in the car at quarter-to-12 for a lunch appointment across town in Mount Govern and there are still lines left over from the weekend laid out on the bedside table so I say fuck it, just this once. Fat fucking chance. The next day it gets started at 8:00 AM. I try holding myself to a couple of lines at a time. Nuh-uh. She won't have it. Mrs. White is a wicked mistress. It reaches the point where kicking off a thousand dollars a week isn't something I question. Instead the logic is: Here he is, the guy with the coke. I want it. I need it. Take the money, however much, but give me that stuff. It's mine. I once go cold turkey. I do it. For a week. For a week I want to die. I say fuck it, it's better to live happily than to kill myself.

Sister Marie Aloysius told me, "Young man, either you believe *in* God, or you've got to believe you *are* God." I'm not saying I think I'm God. I'm just saying I believe in living like I might as well be. There's nobody else as qualified to look out for my own interests as me.

AND HE would have liked very well to have had his fill of pricking that Dolly gal alone, a privy for which he would have shriven his housekeeper with his piece thrown into the garbage.

POTENCY STREET, MONDAY, 10:45 AM

I CALL into the office. "What we got, Dot?"
"A groundbreaking and three grand openings this afternoon. Tonight Mr. Cantare and Mr. Spazini have arranged a private party for you at Wolfswamp." Wolfswamp. Whoopie. Is that tacky, tom-tom-banging, gambling Disneyland the best Cantare could cook up? "Mr. Cantare asked me to tell you that he'll be kind of tied-up in the honeymoon suite, so Mr. Spazini will be hosting you." So now that he's gotten hitched, Hank is dumping me with the Spaz, who when he got washed-up (which if you ask me was around the time of his first bout), became those dumb-ass Injuns' lame-ass excuse for a celebrity endorsement.

"Send Sanchez over in ten minutes, Dotty. And call Nicky and tell her I'll be stopping by for a trim this afternoon."

"Yes, sir."

"Anything else, Dot?"

"Just happy birthday, Mayor."

I hang up, get up, pull the blinds up, and snort up. I'm sixty years old and, as predicted, it's raining in La Plata.

H E OFTEN whacked it over with the village pervert, who was a lurid man, a dropout of Syracuse, and they would ho' long, disgusting ass to who had been the better night erotic, Donaldo of Atlantic City or Sir Hugh of Chicago.

MT. MACREL, MONDAY, 12:00 PM

I HAVE Sanchez swing by the office so in honor of my birthday I can exchange the Cupid for John the Baptist. On the way to the first grand opening I make a little pit-stop. My hand jerks across my chest in a reflex at the entrance. It's a big, dimly lit hall with a line of private booths against the wall. A green light over a door means open for business. Can't smoke in here so I pop a cinnamon lozenge in my mouth. I walk up the aisle and duck behind one of the curtains. A wood panel separating the two sides of the booth slides open onto dark mesh.

"Bless me Padre for I have sinned."

Thought I was talking about a porn shop for a minute, dinja? Hell, these places probably use the exact same set-up on purpose. Makes all those Catholic men with their ice-queen wives feel as at home here in the confession box as they do on the sticky seats at Arousing Superstore. I bet a lot of guys show up both places every week.

On my birthday I have two traditions: confess and get a haircut. Actually, it's more like twice a month I get a trim while I drop in on this establishment maybe every other year, mostly when elections are coming up. I wouldn't call it conscience exactly. It's just that a partial admission every now and then keeps transgression in perspective—especially when the guy you tell it to can't be coerced into telling anybody what you confessed, not even under oath. There's something about Padre Perro I trust, something to do with him being a spic. An Italian priest will take your dirty laundry and turn it into next Sunday's homily. Not Padre Perro.

"It's been a month since my last confession."

"You always say that, Don. And you come here once a year tops. Happy birthday, by the way."

"I thought you weren't supposed to be able to see through that screen."

"I don't need to see. You've got your own special combo of menthols and cough drops."

"Okay, Padre. But your professional oath still stands, correct?"

"Yeah, whatever. But really, Don, what could you possibly tell me I don't already know? Fornication, adultery, gluttony, stealing, onanism, name of the Lord in vain—it's been the same for decades."

"I've got a new one to add to the list."

"Really? How exciting! Murder? No, you'd never kill anybody, Don—at least you'd never admit to it."

"Let's call it . . . lust."

"Lust? That's nothing new for you."

"I'm not talking in the sex sense, and even there I don't really lust. I take care of it. I just jack off or fuck."

"Jesus, Don! This is a church! I'm a priest!"

"Sorry. Fornicated. Masturbated."

"That's better. So what's got you lusting?"

"On second thought, Padre, maybe it's actually idol worship. Yeah, that's more like it. I've been worshipping an idol. Only I'm not willing to say it's a false idol. It's as real as anything I've ever felt in my life."

"What are you talking about, Don? Spit it out."

Something about the way Padre Perro says "spit it out"

makes me swallow the hot cough drop. I say to myself there's no way I should be kneeling here, not now. I think about how much money is in the campaign fund and the fact that there's no limit to mayoral terms in La Plata, not to mention that nobody—at least nobody serious—has run against me in ten years. I can't be kneeling in a confessional. Not yet. Christ, I need a cigarette!

"Forgive me, Padre, but I have to go."

"Oh great, Don! Just like when you last came around."

I get up from the kneeler. "I'll come back another time."

"You know what they say, Don: There might not *be* time."

I push the curtain aside, get out of the booth, and make my way back down the aisle.

Padre Perro's voice echoes in the empty church. "You know it isn't confession if you don't confess!"

BUT **MISTRESS** Nicky, the barber of the same village, was in the habit of saying that no one could come up to the night erotic Barry of DC, and that if anyone could come-pear with him it was Whitey, brother of Willy of Boston, for Bulger was ready for anything—he was none of your finical night erotics, who went around whimpering as his brother did, and in point of vigor he did not flog behind him.

EUCALYPTUS STREET, MONDAY, 5:30 PM

"SANCHEZ, take me to Chevalier's." I snort a few lines on the way for my birthday.

I walk into Nicky's private room, throw my coat on the couch, and sit in the chair in front of the big mirror. Nicky closes the door onto the main salon and lowers the shades on the French doors that open on the garden.

"I need a quick trim."

"Do you have an appointment?" she teases.

"Yeah, with your boss, my old friend Monsieur Chevalier, about your job."

"Don't go bullying me, Pally. Just 'cuz you rent my hands now and then doesn't mean you own my ass."

I grab it, her ass. Give it a good squeeze. "Yeah. That's public domain. Isn't it, Nicky?" She titters and waddles away.

Nicky is the perfect lady barber. She can talk sports and she's kind of sexy in a grotesque way, classic quickie material: big bones, hairy arms, flat chest, fat ass, and an eye-popping mole on her cheek. Every day she wears a foxy gown like she's on her way to the big ball. Some people would say its unappetizing, dressed-up bologna, but I enjoy this Italian staple. Call it antipasto. Eat it once a week.

"Just a little off the sides." Nicky snaps the apron out over me. She tucks tissue into my collar and lifts off John the Baptist, setting it on a Styrofoam head on the shelf. "And dye the moustache while you're at it."

"Don't be silly, Pally, you don't have a moustache."

"I mean your own."

"Jackass!" Nicky grabs a towel and gives me a snap.

I settle into the laminated leather. I get some of my best snoozes here at Chevalier's. All is talcum and Burmasol as I drop off. Ah! I might even have time to take a face rub if that little Filipino faggot is free.

A T LAST, when his tits were gone, besides his hair, he came to conceive the strangest idea that ever occurred to any madman in this world. It now appeared to him fitting and necessary, in order to win a greater amount of hard-ons for himself and perve his country at the same time, to become a night erotic and roam the world on whores' backs, in a suit of Armani; he would go in quest of indentures, by way of putting into practice all that he had seen in his flicks; he would ride every manner of shlong, placing himself in situations of the greatest puerile such as would rebound to the internal glowing of his *ñame*.

EUCALYPTUS STREET, MONDAY, 6:00 PM

I COME around to the fragrant, wet warmth of a faceful of shaving towel. I can tell from the chill creeping up my pant leg that the French doors are open. Nicky must have snuck out to the garden for a smoke while waiting for my pores to dilate.

"Nicky?"

I hear the hinges squeak and the scissors come snip-snipping toward me. She puts a hand on my knee. Hello! I'm thinking, *this is friendlier than usual,* when—Whoa!—the hand moves up my thigh, a turn-on that's really tweaked by the continued snipping of the shears. She starts to unzip my fly. Suddenly— B'gock!—there's her hand over my cock.

"Mm! Come here, you little monkey." I reach for her wrist, dainty and hairy as hell, palms like little paws, fingernails like— Yike!—claws.

"Ook ook! Ai ai ai!"

I jerk my hand away and whip the towel off my face. My zipper is open and there's the white-cheeked gibbon pushing a scissor point against the bulge in my briefs. I can't move. I don't have the wind to yell or jump out of the chair. The gibbon raises the splayed scissors above his head and plunges the blades into my lap, piercing the underwear and exposing Sinatra to the bright lights of the salon. The ape lifts his fist again and is about to finish the job when the door rattles. Nicky enters with a potful of hot foam and the gibbon scrambles out the French doors and into the garden. I leap out of the chair to chase the escaped ape but my pants drop to my ankles and trip me up.

Nicky stares at me in disbelief. "Christ, Pally! Keep it in your pants!"

I'm sprawled on the floor. "Did you fucking see that?"

Nicky shuts the French doors. "Oops. Wind must have blown them open."

I struggle with the trousers and get up. "Nicky, I gotta go."

"What about your hot shave?"

"Bring me the goddamn toupee."

"Don't you want a massage from Paj?"

As REAR-ARDOR for his baller and the might of his arm, the poor fellow could already see himself crowned Pimper of La Plata at the very least; and so, carried away by the strange pleasure that he found in such shots as these, he at once set about putting his flan into erect.

MASHPOTATO NATION, MONDAY, 8:30 PM

SANCHEZ swings me by the mansion and I change my pants before heading across the state line to Wolfswamp. The Mashpotato Indian casino rises out of the trees like Darth Vader's teepee village. I wince every time I see it shining through the windshield. Reminds me of on the way into DC that gay-ass temple set up by the Mormons. *Surrender Dorothy!*

Sanchez drops me off in front of the Grand Mashpotato. "Joo sure joo don Juan me to go een with joo, jorona?"

"Nah. Wait in the parking lot, catch some Zs." I'm not mayor of this place, and even if I were, the Chief Sachem and his warriors wouldn't give a shit about local government. Out here, they play by different rules. After all, this isn't America. This here's Wolfswamp. Mashpotato Nation.

The lobby of the Grand Mashpotato sparkles with crystal and shines with polished brass. I take the glass elevator to the top floor. Stationed outside the entrance to the Spaz's room is a heap-big, stone-faced brave with an earpiece. Dark shades conceal the warpaint. I'd put his jacket size at about sixty. Right when I'm about to turn around and head back down, Geronimo throws open the door and says, "Mr. Spazini is expecting you."

There's nobody in the living room. The spokesgorilla's golden cage is equipped with a wet bar, home theater system, and luxuriant leather furniture. Coon music booms from the stereo and the steaming air stinks of sweat.

"Spaz! Where are you, Spaz?"

A woman's voice: "We're in the bedroom. In the Jacuzzi."

They're in the bedroom in the Jacuzzi: three flavors of whore—a blonde, a black, and an Indian—batting around a tub full of suds and nuzzling each other's bare boobs. Deeper in the whipped cream, wedged between chocolate and strawberry, suckling from a fifth of B&D that vanilla is pouring over her artificial tits, is my friend Donny "the Spaz" Spazini. I haven't finished taking in this Neapolitan sundae when Ray-Ban Crazy Horse enters to dump a packed baggie of white powder on the table. He exits with an *ugh!* The Spaz has briefly passed out, his head swimming in boobs and bubbles. I'm panicking, looking around at all the mirrors and fixtures, when the black hooker blows a palmful of froth up my nose. I sneeze and the Spaz starts to come around. His gaze zips up the wall and across the ceiling and his eyes cross when the phantom fly he's following comes crashing down on the peaks of the blonde's silicone mountains. The Spaz shudders and finally levels dilated pupils on me. "Happy birthday, Pally!" I smack him with the back of my hand. "Hey! What was that for?"

"Jesus, Spaz! Are you insane? Have you ever heard of the FBI? I'm set up better than Barry!" Somewhere in a honeymoon suite, Cantare is taking care of his sweet-assed bride. I pick up the phone and ask for his room.

"Happy birthday, boss."

"What the fuck were you thinking, Hank? Any mirror might hide a camera! Every lamp could conceal a microphone!"

"You're paranoid, Pally. This is Wolfswamp. The rooms are debugged every day. The maids vacuum and then they really sweep."

"What about the cunts?"

From the bath, the Spaz pipes up, "They won't say anything, Pally."

"Oh yeah? How do you know, you dumb fuck?"

The Spaz looks at me pityingly. "They'd be fired."

Pocahontas chimes in, "Dincha ever see *Godfather II?*"

I cup the mouthpiece. "Listen, Hank, some fucked-up shit has been happening. That goddamn gibbon is after me."

"Come on, boss, don't go off on that whole monkey-on-your-back rant. Today's your birthday. Tomorrow you can go cold turkey."

"Not monkey, asshole: ape. The white-cheeked gibbon you let out of the zoo. Last night he tried to burn my balls off and this afternoon he wanted to chop off my cock. I thought these fuckers weren't supposed to have thumbs!"

"Pally, you're wigging out."

"Fuck you! It's true!"

"Listen, boss, the top floor of the Grand Mashpotato is completely hermetic. There's round-the-clock security at all the elevators and stairs because of all the cash guests keep in the rooms. Go ahead and have a good time."

Everyone is getting out of the tub and the naked hookers are toweling off the Spaz's muscular ass. He grabs the coke from the coffee table and starts huffing straight from the bag.

"You better be sure about this, Hank."

"You have a nice birthday party up there, boss. I'm going to get back to my wife."

"Go fuck yourself, Hank." I hang up. The Spaz gives the whores a break and stands at the bar swigging from a bottle of nice champagne and fiddling with a lighter and a spoon. He's got a box of baking soda. The Spaz is so absorbed in his little science project that I wonder if he's noticed there's an Indian kid no older than twelve standing in the corner gawking at him. "Planning on baking a cake, Spaz?"

The Spaz doesn't look up. "Yeah. Baking."

"Who's the kid?"

"Chief's nephew. I'm his idol."

The Spaz scribbles a shopping list for the kid to take down to the casino kitchen: tin foil, a straw, more champagne. With the kid out of the way, the Spaz taps some cocaine and baking soda together in the spoon and dribbles on a little water. He flicks the lighter and holds the flame under the spoon for a minute until the stuff gets bubbling.

"Don't tell me you're going to swallow that crap."

"Nah. This just increases the potency."

"What's the matter with you, Spaz! Is this that jigaboo shit?"

"Nope. Spades use ether."

The Indian kid returns with the bubbly, a soda straw, and an industrial-sized box of aluminum foil. The Spaz gives the kid a whack with the roll of wrap. "We're not building a UFO, you little dipshit!" The Spaz tears off a small square and taps the spoon out onto it.

"Uh, Spaz?"

"Yeah, Pally?"

I nod in the direction of the kid. "Are you sure he should be watching this?"

The Spaz looks right through him. "Who? What?"

"The kid. What you're doing."

"Oh. Don't worry, Pally. He won't say anything. Watch this. Hey, kid, did you hear the one about the ventriloquist driving through the desert? He pulls up to Big Chief's Last Chance Gas, right? Says to Big Chief, 'Fill 'er up, and while you're at it do you mind if I talk with the horse?' 'Go 'head, dumb paleface,' says Big Chief. Ventriloquist goes over and says to the horse, 'Say, Mr. Horse, what's it like living here at Big Chief's Last Chance Gas?' And the horse says, 'The desert is too hot and Big Chief leaves me tied up in the sun without any water.' Big Chief says, 'Ugh! Horse never talk before . . .' Ventriloquist says, 'Say,

Big Chief, do me a favor and check the oil, and if it's all right I'll go chat with the dog.' Big Chief says, 'Go 'head, crazy white man.' Ventriloquist walks up to the dog and says, 'Say, Mr. Dog, what's it like living here on the edge of the desert at Big Chief's Last Chance Gas?' Dog says, 'I don't get nothing to eat and every now and then Big Chief comes over and gives me a big kick for no reason.' Big Chief says, 'Ugh! Dog never talk before.' So the Ventriloquist says, 'Wash the windshield, Big Chief, and while you're at it, is it okay if I speak with the sheep?' Big Chief hollers, 'No!—'"

The Spaz starts laughing so hard he almost chokes on his own snot. It takes him a minute to recover before he can deliver Big Chief's big line.

"'Sheep lie!'"

The Indian kid doesn't laugh or cry. He doesn't say anything. He stares at us with the dumbest look I've ever seen. It's not that he's angry or simply doesn't get it. He just stands there like a totem pole adoring the Spaz, who finishes his hilarity fit with a big farmer's blow right in the middle of the carpet.

"What? Is he retarded?"

"Uh-huh. Mute, too." The Spaz upends the bottle and takes a swig of champagne.

The coke and soda has crystallized into a glittering little pile of rocks and my mouth starts watering. The whores are snoring. I consider the surveillance sterility of the suite, the huge scout posted outside the door, the kid's disability, and the Spaz's loyalty—or better put, his zero-credibility after eating so much mat. In this corner, weighing in at 185 pounds, former middleweight but never champion Donny "the Spaz" Spazini, mouth open, tongue drooping like stuffing from the punching bag his head has become, having trouble peeling paper off a soda straw with his enormous, arthritic hands. "Give me that."

I tear off the paper, shove the plastic tip up my nose, and bend over the cooked-down coke.

"Uh, Pally, that's not where it goes."

I pull the straw out of my nose. "Well, where the fuck am I supposed to stick it?"

"You heat the foil until the stuff starts to smoke. The straw's like a pipe. It goes in your mouth."

"You learn this from those jungle bunnies you cocksuck?"

"Yeah—I mean, no!" The Spaz's single eyebrow knits in his me-angry look. "Look, Pally, I don't suck nobody's cock."

"Forget it, Spaz. Give me a light."

I put the straw between my lips and the Spaz waves the lighter, cranked up to the highest flame, underneath the foil. He huddles close to help me get it cooking and the rocks melt with a *snap popple crack!* It doesn't smell like coke, but then again what does coke smell like? Dead nasal tissue? I lean in close to sip the acrid little plume of smoke. I hold it in my lungs. It tastes like shit, and then on second thought it tastes like heaven. I look up at the Spaz and his eyes are watering from the fumes, but in that moment it might as well be out of heartbreaking tenderness toward me. I'm grateful enough for this instant kick—in one breath I go from *a second ago I didn't know about this and if it hadn't been for the Spaz I might never have tried it*, to *now I can't live without it*—that I'd like to kiss him. In a brotherly way? In a romantic way? Hard to say. I mean, hell, this is better than sex. This is orgasm. And it's lasting longer than three seconds. I'm holding heaven in my lungs and all of the sudden the Spaz does something that takes my breath away. He cradles the back of my skull like a lover and pulls me toward him. I close my eyes, reach out my hand, and steady myself against his massive barrel chest. I feel the Spaz's muscular tongue thrust itself into my mouth. Our lips lock, and with the vacuous force of his lungs filling up, the Spaz sucks the wind right out of me. He releases his hand and I collapse into his chest. My eyelids slowly part, lips remain parted. We're eyeball-to-eyeball, the Spaz and I, my chin against his solar plexus. He holds his breath and wheezes, "Can't waste this shit." The Spaz exhales sweet, putrid smoke back into my face, when all of a sudden over his shoulder the Indian kid is lunging at us with a savage frown, clutching the champagne bottle like a club. I'm frozen gripping the straw and the foil, but the Spaz sees the terror in my eyes and reflex-spins with an iron fist. Three things happen in less time than it took the smoke to get me high out of my homophobic underwear: My head gets sprayed with champagne, the Spaz lands the kid a left hook, and the little retard is laid flat, coldcocked. The buzz lifts quicker than you can say, *Pryor puffed a plague of Parkinson's.*

The Spaz shakes a bruise off his knuckles and whimpers, "The coke is soaked!" The fizzled rocks are floating in a pond of Perignon.

"That little retard tried to scalp me!"

The Spaz looks up with a Curious-George-clueless grin. "Wow, Pally! There's smoke coming out of your ear!"

The Spaz checks the kid's vitals while I go into the bathroom to remove the toupee and towel off. Strange: The hairpiece is now slightly shorter on one side and the ends are gnarled and melted. It takes me a minute in the mirror to put it all together. I go back in the living room and notice a pungent odor in the air. The Spaz presses his ear against the Indian kid's chest. Retarded little shit saved my skull. In his right hand, the Spaz still has a thumb on the lever of the leaking lighter. I hear the butane hissing. The Spaz turns and his big, sqaure jaw goes slack.

"Holy shit! Pally? That you?" It's the first time he's seen me without the wig. "You look like a monkey!"

"Yeah? I smell like one too." I kick the Spaz's ass. Hard.

"Ow! What was that for?"

"For torching John the Baptist."

We get a bellhop to bring the retarded kid down to the casino doctor, a quack they keep on call for the occasional lose-your-shirt heart attack. Tell him the kid was playing leapfrog with the champ when he caught a brass doorknob in the chin.

THE FIRST thing he did was to burnish up some old pieces of Armani left to him by his great-grandfather, which for ages had lain in a corner, moldering and forgotten. He brushed and altered them as best he could, and then he noticed that one very important thing was lacking: There was no hair on his head, but only a bare cranium or polished forehead, with combed-over bangs of the kind shoe shiners use. His ingenuity, however, enabled him to remedy this, and he proceeded to fashion out of horsebrush a kind of half-hairmat, which, when attached to the moron, gave the appearance of a whole one.

MASHPOTATO NATION, MONDAY, 9:15 PM

I TAKE one of the razor blades the Spaz uses for chopping his complimentary coke and scrape off John the Baptist's singed fringe. I fish in my jacket pocket for the smart-guy glasses. Tortoise-shell frames cover up the mutilated sideburn. The Spaz wakes up the whores and lines all three up on the side of the bed, legs spread. He gets down on his hands and knees like a cowboy laying an ambush. You know the chemical formula can't be too different from novocaine, the way the Spaz doesn't seem to realize he's drooling. He munches back and forth down the row like corn-on-the-cob. While blonde and squaw keep up their exaggerated moans, black beauty says to me, "As long as you're here in this room, anything goes." She arches her back in a crab-walk, pushing her big muff into the Spaz's nose. "Anything."

The Spaz comes up for air, butter all over his face and tassels in his teeth. "Pussy, Pally?"

"I'll pass, Spaz." I opt for the cocaine instead, scooping some up in the spoon to go snort in the living room. I sit down on the leather couch and grab the remote. While the Spaz chin-surfs the sluts, I channel-surf the premium porno.

TRUE, WHEN he went to see if it was strong enough to withstand a good trashy blow, he was somewhat disjointed; for when he drew his gourd and gave it a couple of thrusts, he sucked seed only in ungluing a whore's weak labor. The sleaze with which he had screwed it to tits disturbed him no piddle, and he decided to jake it over. This time he placed a few flicks of porn on the vid's eye, and then, convinced that it was strong enough, refrained from pulling it to any further teets; instead, he copped it then and there as the finest hairmat ever laid.

MASHPOTATO NATION, MONDAY, 9:30 PM

I FIND a movie that I have in my home collection, but it looks even better on HDTV. "*Troop Sex!*" I'm watching this video for the umpteenth time. The cheesy music makes me want to scream. And yet I've just. Got. To watch. "Starring . . ." The pause is too long, a trademark of these flicks, buying time with tortoise-crawl credits. ". . . Dolly Dellabutta!" I tap my balls gently with two fingers, thinking, *like two almonds*.

It's supposed to be a scout pack but they're grown men in green shorts with medals for marksmanship and campfire-making on their shirts. One of them, holding the keys to the mini-van, announces, "I'll drive." Another cries, "Shotgun!" Enter Dolly, dressed in short-short house dress with deep-deep cleavage and—unh!—an apron. She purrs, "I'll take the back-seat." By the second scene they're tying her up with seat belts.

AFTER THIS, he went down to have a look at his wag; and although the animal had more verrugas, or warts, on its hood than there are dimes in a dollar, and more blemishes than gonorrhea's scree which *tantum pellis et ossa fuit,* it nonetheless looked to its master like a far better frank than Clarence's Bocephus or the Baby Face of the Don. He spent all of four decades in trying to kink up a *ñame* for his mount; for—so he told himself—seeing that it belonged to so flaming and warty a night erotic, there was no reason why it should not have a *ñame* of equal renown. The kind of *ñame* he wanted was one that would at once indicate what the frank had been before it came to belong to a night erotic and what its present status was for; for it stood to reason that, when the master's woody condition changed, his hose also ought to have a heinous, thigh-pounding appendage, one suited to the new order of lings and the new perversion that was to follow.

FANTASY AVENUE, MONDAY, 11:00 PM

THE minivan is weaving all over the road and Sanchez flashes the lights to pull them over. When he brings Stella Cantare back to the car, he's got her by the arm, holding it tight.

"You're hurting me!"

"Sanchez, you jackass, can't you see the lady's in distress?"

"But jorona—"

"Shut up. I'll deal with the den mother. You go back to the minivan and take care of those hairless pricks."

Stella gets in beside me and Sanchez shuts the door. Stella and I are alone in the backseat. The hem of her skirt is twisted up over her knees and the place where her sweaty thighs meet the leather upholstery makes a squeaking sound. She wears perfume, a den mother's perfume. The scent has been activated by the struggle. Her khaki blouse barely conceals the white lace bra. When she heaves a great sigh the top button bursts and I get a peek at her cleavage. Stella bursts into tears. "They used the granny knot on me!"

"There there." I smooth back her mussed hair. "Did those little shits hurt you?"

"I'm okay. Just a little shaken up." Through the windshield I see the scouts all fumble for IDs. I lift up the armrest and scoot closer to Stella. My hand is up on her headrest. I let it slide to her shoulders. In reflex, Stella snuggles in. A stray curl dangles down over Stella's wet eyes and she tucks it behind her ear. "They're usually such good boys."

"You know how it is, Stella. Boys turn into teenagers."

That makes Stella think of something. "This reminds me of my first time." She smiles a faraway smile.

"What about it?"

Stella tilts her head back and stares up at the felted ceiling. My hand is on her bare neck. "It was in the backseat. At a drive-in movie. A car a lot like this."

Stella's collar slips down off her shoulder and I run a finger along the strap of her bra. "Must have been a rich kid."

"His dad ran a funeral parlor. All hands. Girls used to call him The Undertaker."

My hand moves down the back of Stella's shirt. All three scouts are spread-eagle against the back of the minivan. Sanchez pulls the blackjack from his belt and whacks one. Must have made fun of his accent. The kid crumples to the pavement and the other scouts bend to help him, but two quick kicks and they're back humping the bumper. Sanchez returns the black-jack to his belt, grabs one of the scouts left standing, and twists the kid's arm behind his back so high his head tilts back and mouth snaps open. He's a starving baby bird trying to cry for Mama but too weak to make a sound. Sanchez trips him and forces his face in the dirt, holding him pinioned with the heel of his boot.

"What movie?"

"It was a double feature. First was *Butch Cassidy*."

I tuck my hand in Stella's armpit and caress along the valley where the side ribs meet the tit. In one easy movement Sanchez slips the big nightstick out of his belt and spins the last scout around. Sanchez raises the stick. The scout's legs are quaking and his hands cover his head. A dark spot spreads across the front of his shorts.

"That's a good one. How about the feature?"

Stella looks up at me with those big, moist eyes and purposefully lays a hand on my lap. "We didn't watch the feature." Sanchez gives it to the kid in the belly and Stella spins away and lifts her skirt. "We made our own movie . . ." No panties, just bearded clam and glorious ass. Just like Dolly Dellabutta's ass. *That ass that ass that ass.* The scouts are all on the ground. Sanchez is kicking them, shouting at them to get up. Face pressed against the headrest, Stella reaches back and yanks open my fly. Bracing herself against the frontseat, she sticks Rock Sinatra in her butter churn. I grab Stella's tits and she rides us into the sunset.

AFTER HE in his memory and imagination had played up, struck out, and discharged many *ñames*, now adding to and now subtracting from the fist, he finally hit upon "Rock Sinatra," a *ñame* that impressed him as being dongerous and at the same time indicative of what the steed had been when it was but a frank, whereas now it was nothing other than the first and foremost of all the franks in the world.

MASHPOTATO NATION, TUESDAY, 8:00 AM

TITS turn into stiff pricks, a dirty trick. I've been pulling on them for more than a minute. Stiff pricks turn into gargantuan tits, the kind that flap and flutter around your ears when the dancer squats to the bar and lets you stick your nose in the fragrant cleft of her chest.

I wake up on the living room couch with come in my hair and my dick hanging out. On the glass tabletop, a glob of fresh semen gunks up the little mound of coke I left myself for breakfast. Fuck! Now it's too goopy to snort. Can't wait for it to dry out. I daub up some of the powdery paste and lick my finger tips. Not bad. Hell, it's good enough for the girls at the strip clubs, and down the hatch works as well as up the nose, just comes on a little slower. I lap the stuff up. Better not to waste this shit.

I tuck in Rock Sinatra and put on my tattered toupee. The Spaz and his whores all snore in the bedroom, so I pull out a twenty, fold myself a little pile of Navajo blow, and show myself out.

In the parking lot of the Grand Mashpotato, Sanchez is asleep in the driver's seat. I tap the glass. When Sanchez wipes the condensation off the inside of the windshield and sees me, his face breaks right into a grin. He starts the car and lowers his window. "Goo moaning, jorona! Hab a heppy berfday?"

"Yeah. Sure. Let's get the hell out of here."

I do five lines to steady myself in the backseat. After a bender like this, I can sometimes feel like shit. I've got to get back to the city. Sometimes my job is all that saves me. Like the freak in *Scanners* who hides inside a huge plaster head and says, "My art keeps me sane," for me it's the same, only instead of art, it's being mayor.

On the outskirts of town there's a sign for my favorite store. I've got three Gs from Three Zs' tow fees, so I decide to buy myself a little birthday present. "Sanchez, pull over up here!"

"De woods, jorona? Joo gotta pee?"

"No, asshole. The parking lot."

I stumble in and post Sanchez near the entrance. There's hair everywhere. Toupees grace every inch of wall space. The proprietor, falling asleep in a comic book, wears an awful mop. Even the dog, a Chihuahua curled up in himself on a pillow on the floor, snoozes with a bad little hairmat strapped to his skull, late-Elvis sideburns tied beneath his chin.

I spot my new model in a dirty glass showcase. It's a homely little nutty-professor number and the color is a little different from my regular, but something about it speaks to me. Maybe it's the sparkle of silver that makes it look distinguished. I can have Nicky tint me to match. I lift the lid on the case and the size checks out, so I take the hairpiece to the front and give the proprietor the money. The drowsy dog jumps to its feet, yapping spastically when it gets a whiff of what his master's putting in a box. "Easy, Fabian," the wigmaster coos. He winks at me. "This one makes him feisty."

HAVING FOUND a *ñame* for his frank that pleased his fancy, he then desired to do as much for himself, and this required another tweak, and by the end of that period he had made up his mind that he was henceforth to be boned as Don "Pally" Dimaio.

MACNAMARA PLAZA, TUESDAY, 11:00 AM

I GO into City Hall, pour myself a glass of press conference water, and buzz Dot. "What we got?"

"Four ribbon-cuttings this afternoon and tonight the new show opens at La Plata Dramatic Arts Network. They sent over tickets for the gala reception."

"What is it?"

"A black-tie shindig with a lot of booze."

"No, I mean what's the show?"

"Oh. Carla Chong in *Hello! Cholly!*"

"Carla Chong in *Hello! Cholly!?*"

"Carla Chong in *Hello! Cholly!* Do you want to go?"

What do you know! Carla Chong in *Hello! Cholly!* I'm thinking I might not mind meeting the gal. Carla fucking Chong! When I was a boy I used to fantasize about her slanty bug eyes blinking up at me from the TV while she cracked jokes with Porkloin, that piggy puppet. Just the memory of it makes Sinatra twitch. Carla Chong was probably my first television hard-on. Maybe she's my hope for Rock's comeback. "Yeah, Dotty, I'll go. Tell the pricks at LaPDAN I'll present Chong with a special citation from the city. Call tomorrow Carla Chong Day."

"Yes, Mayor. I'll have a certificate drawn up."

"And make an appointment with Nicky for Friday."

I'll wait until the end of the week to try out my new head-dress. Best to introduce big changes like dye jobs when the prick columnists from the *PlaGa* have the day off. I go over to the bar, press the button, and open the secret compartment. What'll it be to meet Mrs. C? Let's make it the mighty Ducktail.

A ND SO, having polished up his rubber and made the moronic closed hairmat, and having given his hose a *ñame*, he naturally found but one thing whacking still: He must seek out an old lady who could become a mistress; for a night erotic without an old lady is like a latrine without pees or poops, a booty without a hole.

LAPDAN, TUESDAY, 10:00 PM

BACKSTAGE at the La Plata Dramatic Arts Network I'm chain-smoking. I've got to watch how I handle this one in front of the press and the various hangers-on in the house. I don't give a shit about speculation, but it could be a little ridiculous if they get me saying anything sexy to the old broad's beat-up face. Seeing her in the stage lights makes Sinatra wiggle a little. Back when I was just a punk kid on *Child's Play*, whacking off to Carla Chong in that rat's nest of a harlot wig singing "Gold Is a Dame's Greatest Pal," who would have thought I'd someday get the chance to make the old dame suck me off in person?

I'm waiting in the wings for the show to end when up comes a little prick with a sniveling voice. "Pardon me, but I can't have you smoking here in the backstage area." You can't have me? You bet your gay ass you can't have me! Who does this prick think he is? I smile and turn away, thinking that will be it, but the prick persists. "I'm sorry but you'll have to put that out."

"Goddamn right you're sorry. Sanchez, who is this prick?"

"Ehstage mana, jorona."

The stage manager grabs my elbow. I wheel around and here's this homo in my face. Does he know who I am? "I know you're the mayor, but if you're going to have to keep smoking you'll have to go outside on the loading dock."

So I say it. I say it somewhere between *get your hands off me* and *shithead* and *prick* and *wherever you eat in this town I'll make sure the chef tells his Puerto Rican dishwasher to piss in your soup.* It doesn't matter that I say *shithead* or *prick,* those float away like smoke. It's *faggot* that squishes like a turd right under this guy's mental shoe, and so he throws a hissy and has the reporters from the *La Plata Gazette* writing it in their little stenos. Turns out faggot LaPDAN stage manager is faggot friends with the faggot *PlaGa* arts editor. Carla Chong hears about the snit fit and calls what I said "hate speech." Bitch. "Fine with me," I tell the pricks from the paper, "because I wasn't looking forward to hanging out with that has-been." Geriatric cunt probably would have drooled on me.

Back at the mansion I take off the duck's ass and unwind with a long, hot bath. When I get out of the tub and wipe the condensation off the mirror, another pair of eyes look back at me in the reflection. Over my shoulder in the bathroom window an animal is showing me its hairy little ass. I reach in the closet for the towels, the top stack I tell Oprah never to touch, pull out the pistol, swing around, and blast one off. The glass shatters with the explosion and there's a terrible screech. The bullet hits the little fucker and—*p'ting!*—ricochets off the window frame and whizzes between my legs just under my bare scrotum. My pubes are fucking smoking! Fuck! Even in his death throes that goddamn gibbon manages to moon me and shave my balls!

I knock out the broken glass with the butt of the gun, crane my head through the window frame, and see the little corpse. I got him! I blew the head off the fucking gibbon! Only for some reason the decapitated gibbon has the body of a cat. The neighbor's cat.

Oprah calls, "Y'all okay, Mayo?"

"I'm fine!" I shout. "It was just a light bulb!"

I F," HE sprayed to himself, "as a powder-sniff for my quims or by a smoke of good poultice I should come upon some agent hereabouts, a thing that very commonly happens to night erotics, and if I should spray him in a hand-to-hand encunter or perhaps cut him in two, or, finally, if I should banquet and fondue him, would it not be well to have someone to whom I may send him as a pheasant, in order that he, if he is sieving, may come in, fall upon his knees in front of my sweet old lady, and spray in a humble and submissive bone of vice, 'I, lady, am the giant Giuliani, Lord of the Island of Manhattan, who has been overcome in single kumquat by that night erotic who never can aspirate enough, Don Dimaio of La Plata, the same who sent me to pheasant myself before your mace that your heiney-ass may dispose of me as you see fit'?" Oh, how our good night erotic reveled in this peach, and more than ever when he came to think of the *ñame* that he should give his lady!

BELFRY STREET, WEDNESDAY, 5:00 PM

ANOTHER full day of ribbon cuttings while burning through the coke I borrowed from the Spaz. A gooey mix of bloody snotrags and menthol butts stews in the ashtray when I see the prick publisher of the *PlaGa* and his wife coming out of Café Nova. "Sanchez, slow down!" I pop the nasty ashtray out of its slot and power down the window. "Hey! Sukoff! Skimp on your wife's dessert again?" He knows my car. Everybody in La Plata does. Sukoff reaches for his wife's arm. The fairy is scared! Chickenshit muckraker thinks I'm going to shoot him or something, as if I'd be goombah enough to try and get away with a plain-day drive-by. Patronizing prick! Pisses me off so much I go ahead and wind up. The loaded brush raised over my head, I'm Jacksoff Polack and the whole art world's behind me. I summon all my strength and sling. I'm a good shot from throwing all those first pitches over so many little-league seasons—more than any other mayor—and a second later Sukoff is spitting bloody ash and his hot-tempered wife's got sputum-soaked cotton nubs splattered across her dress. That'll melt that icicle up her ass! Sukoff is already on his cell assigning the shocking story to one of his non-union stooges at the *PlaGa* meanwhile dictating an enraged idiotorial that's supposed to pass as the opinion of the whole soulless paper. He's bullying his Jew country-club buddies from the networks to lead with this bit at 6 and 11, looping dramatic pans of the misses' drecked dress while the mic-mongers hound me for a comment. But when I look out the back window and see the pale publisher and his charity-circuit battle-ax retreating as a blank canvas, I realize I'm still holding the loaded brush and that a supernatural gravity pulls me back. Eyes on the road as we coast through the stop sign to Macnamara Plaza, Sanchez steers with one hand while the other holds a firm grip on my wrist.

"Shithead spic," I spit, slackening my wind-up. "I had a clear shot."

As the story goes, there was a very good-looking baller who lived nearby, with whom he had once been smitten, although it is generally believed that her husband never knew or suspected it. Her name was Stella Cantare, and it seemed to him that she was the one upon whom he should bestow the title of mistress of his shots.

PROFIT STREET, WEDNESDAY, 6:00 PM

ANOTHER one of these fucking campaign cocktails where the host doesn't know his ass from a bottle. Hank and his wife arrive fresh off their honeymoon. "Hi, boss," says Cantare, "How'd you like your birthday treat?"

"The Spaz is such an ass. He nearly fricasseed me. I had to buy a new fucking rug. Say, Hank, lend me five bills, will you?"

"You know I never say no, boss, but don't you think you've got to curb the spending some?"

I pull Hank nearer to a stereo blaring canned classical. "What is this bullshit, Hank? Don't you snort my blow up your nose? Don't you eat free on my name? Don't you buy your wife's fucking Amazonian furniture off the fat of my city?"

"I'm not saying moderation, Pally. You just have to make smart choices about how you use money."

"I come out behind some days, but in the long run you can bet I'm going to get ahead. Think of my autobiography. That'll be an easy million. And then the movie they'll make of me. Who do you think will play you? Sorvino?"

"Too fat."

"Pesci."

"Too short."

"Liotta?"

The smile on Cantare's face says *just right*. "Right, Liotta.

Now would you pretty-fucking-please lend me five hundred bucks?" He pulls out his clip and forks over five bills.

While Hank is busy with his greetings, I push a stiff martini into Stella's fist and steer her into the solarium. Something in Stella's drowsy, squinty face is growing on me. She's the only woman here with more than air between her ears. Stella looks at me with big, hot, sad eyes, the kind that melt ice cubes. When I jiggle my whiskey a little splashes onto my suit pants and I feel the chilly trickle deep down in the cuff of my briefs. "Hello, Mrs. Cantare. How's life as the trophy wife?"

"Just fine." Stella stands close and brushes my hairy knuckles with the back of her hand. It's a delicate, birdlike hand, but I bet it sure knows how to grab a guy's balls. "How's life as the city pimp?"

Sassy. I'm ready to talk dirty with her for a while when the cocksucker host interrupts. It makes me feel like killing someone the way he stands there blabbering and staring at me with my empty glass. He makes me shake the dry ice and ask for a refill. I excuse myself to the kitchen like I need a moment of mayoral reflection, find a half-empty jar of Dimaio's Own Mayonnaise in the fridge, and sneak it into the john with me. Visions of Stella's ass still fresh in my retina, I jack off into the jar. Back in the kitchen I fish in the sink for a dirty fork and stir up the dressing. I screw the cap back on the jar and put My Own Mayo back in the fucking refrigerator.

I ditch the party and have Sanchez swing me by Mer de Tyranno, where three bills from Hank's loan gets Dylan to refill my prescription for another eight-ball.

FOR HER he wished a *ñame* that should not be incongruous with his own and that would convey the suggestion of a pimpèd or a date lady; and accordingly, he resolved to ball her "Stella Dellabutta," she being related to that ass. A juiciful *ñame* to his rear, out of the ordinary and significant, like the others he had hosen for himself and his appendage.

POTENCY STREET, THURSDAY, 10:00 AM

PARADE day. I get up and do a few lines from the fresh bindle, go into the bathroom, and open the box from the toupee store to try on my salt-and-pepper special. Color's a little off, but the wig fits like magic. I run a comb through my new hair. When someone says, "Good Morning, Don Dimaio!" I almost jump out of my skin.

"What the fuck!"

"I'm the Hairpiece of Heroditus!" The voice—Hackett's yap meets Delouise's wheeze—is as close as the mirror. I crack the medicine cabinet. Nothing but pills and shave cream.

"Hank, that you?"

"Bonaparte's middle part!"

I whip open the closet and push aside the robes and towels. "Come out of there, jackass!"

"A.k.a. the coonskin cap on the minuteman who shot the last Hessian!"

"What the fuck is going on here?"

From the hall, Oprah calls, "Y'all want something, Mayo?"

"No!"

"Keep your voice down, Don Dimaio. I can hear you fine and you're the only one who can hear me."

"Where the hell are you?"

"Right on top of your skull."

I take off the toupee and the chatter stops, but when I put

it back on the rant is up and running: "Washington's wig! De Tocqueville's toup! Hitler's comb-over! Cleaver's beaver! No joke, I've got a hair from each."

"I don't fucking believe this."

"You're not hallucinating, if that's what you think. You, Don Dimaio, are the lucky new owner of the world's one and only enchanted wig, the sentient, astral-traveling toupee of ages— but you can just call me Rug."

"Jesus Christ!"

"Never humped his head, but certain miracles do come to him who wears me." Either I'm on the wiggiest narcotics trip since Lynch's talking asshole typewriter or the FBI's more demented than when they tried passing Castro the poisoned pen: a hugged rug. I lean close to the mirror and feel through the fibers for a transmitter. "Watch it! Hey! You're worrying my weave!"

"Where'd they put the fucking thing?"

"There's no wire, no electronics whatsoever. I'm nothing but natural fibers. You won't find a hair out of place."

"This is too fucked up!" I think I'm joking when I add, "When do I get my three wishes?"

"Actually, Don Dimaio, it's just one wish."

"No shit?"

"And it's pretty specific. You get to choose a person to drive."

"Huh?"

"Comes with the hairitory. Ha! That's a joke. But seriously, Don Dimaio, you can select somebody to take over from time to time. That's what makes me magical. You twist me backwards on your head and teleport anywhere, across town or around the world, and get under someone else's skin. You've got to pick the person wisely, because once it's done it can't be undone until my next possession."

"I can choose anybody in the world?"

"Yup. But I should tell you what's worked best for my owners over the years. Make it someone close to you. Keep him loyal. Collect—and even create!—dirt on him . . . Well, Don Dimaio, who do you want to remote-control?"

"Shut up a minute, all right? Let me think."

"Pick a body, any body."

I could choose a made man, a Matriarca with a lot of cash, and make him give it to me. But the sight of blood makes me queasy, plus money's not really a problem as long as I have this job, and I've got a pretty good idea the cards have been dealt so that I'll have this job for a good, long time. If this thing is for real, then it probably should go to somebody whose movements I already kind of control. Somebody I send around on mayoral errands who it might make sense for me to spy on from time to time. Somebody so loyal he might eventually run the risk of becoming a stoolie or a Brutus. Somebody whose testimony I would want to control, if it ever came to that. Somebody like Cantare, my director of administration, the one guy close enough to ever finger me. After all, he's been acting funny lately, bitching at me about money and sending freaks like Fritos to see me.

"And I get to control the guy completely?"

"Head to toe—and everything in between."

Finally, what my decision comes down to is, *Christ! I'd like to fuck Cantare's wife!* "Let's make it Hank Cantare."

"Abracadabra, Don Dimaio!" The Rug lets out a little puff of smoke. "Cantare it will be!"

FART **II**: *Which treats of the first Stella that the 'gina man Don Dimaio made with his satyr wreath.*

Having, then, made all these desecrations, he did not wish to lose any time in pulling his flan into erect, for he could not but come himself for the girl what he was losing by his decay, so many were the shlongs that were to be righted, the beaver pants to be undressed, the cute bushes to be done away with, and the hooties to be perfora'd. Accordingly, without informing anyone of his perversion and without letting anyone see him, he set out one morning before daybreak on one of those very cold days in November.

MACNAMARA PLAZA, THURSDAY, 3:00 PM

CANTARE, Stella, and I are bundled into the back of a convertible. The Rug wanted to come along but my dyed-black sides don't yet match its silvery luster, so I wear the Brushcut instead. Stella rides in between. I like the feel of her thigh against mine. I'm throwing the papal wave with one hand and massaging Sinatra with the other, imagining what it's going to be like to get up in Stella's caboose, when suddenly the motorcade has to stop so Cantare can run to the bathroom. "What da matter?" I say to Stella. "Hank got a wittle-boy bladder?"

I expect Stella to oblige with some third-grade pitter-patter, but instead she says straight-faced, "Actually, Pally, I was rubbing his cock under the blanket. He couldn't stand it anymore and had to go finish the job." Cantare comes back from the Port-o-John and his complexion is flushed like that's exactly what happened. When Stella climbs out of the car at the finish I take a close look. I can't detect a panty line through her tight-fitting dress. By the looks of things she's probably got on nothing underneath, or maybe a thong. *Gong!* Sinatra shimmies.

After the parade, Hank and I press the flesh while Stella goes home to stuff the bird. They know I've got nobody to do the turkey with, so Hank and Stella have invited me over to their place. Sanchez drives Cantare and me across the city line to Hank's mansion in Crampton. Cantare says, "You want a toot before we go inside?"

Of course I do, but if Hank does a few too he'll still be hyper after dinner. "No, Hank, this night's something special for your new bride. Booze will do."

Stella puts together a nice table and looks fine as hell in a short wool skirt that rides almost to her ass. I'm expected to say some kind of prayer because I'm the mayor. "Let's be thankful for our health, family, and education. Let's be thankful for spirit. They can never take away our spirit. Now carve the goddamn turkey, Hank."

Every time Stella bends over to scoop on more stuffing I get a look up the back of the skirt. I take seconds and thirds and get the shadow of her shelf in eyefuls, meanwhile refilling Cantare's glass four times with red wine to leave him primed. Stella gets up to warm dessert and Hank excuses himself to the living room. When I check on him he's konked out on the couch with a brass floor lamp shining over his head. I flick the switch. "Night, loverboy."

In the kitchen, Stella, in short skirt and rubber gloves, rinses plates and bends to put them in the dishwasher. *Madonn'!* The water must be simmering! "Thanks for dinner, Stella. Hank fell asleep, so—"

"Aw! He passed out before the best part! Well, you'll still stay for a slice of pie, *woncha*, Pally?"

I wouldn't mind getting down right in the suds. She's got a big, sweet ass under that skirt she wears and I want to grab it. But what if Sinatra is too shy to sing? Focus, Pally, focus. "Sorry to eat and run, Stella, but I've got some business to attend to in town."

At the door, Stella gives me a peck on the forehead. "Happy Thanksgiving, Pally."

"Sanchez, get me home in a hurry." There's nobody on the roads and by the time I've laid out and lapped up five lines, Sanchez has made it back to the mayoral mansion. "Tell me, Pancho, you spics celebrate today?"

"Chore," says Sanchez, "ebry day een America we say sanku."

"Well, take the rest of the night off. Go be with your fucking people."

"*¡Gracias, jorona!*"

I scramble around my bedroom and get everything I need: cognac, Vaseline, remote control, lines laid out on the bedside table. I lie down and put on the Rug.

"I don't know what you think you'll need that jar of jelly for, Don Dimaio. This is going to be much better than a video. And it won't be your run-of-the-mill projection either. Have you ever had an OBE?"

"You mean like the award for daytime TV?"

"No. *Oh-be-ee*: out-of-body experience."

"Oh. I don't think so."

"How about sleep paralysis? Right at the edge of waking up, when you can't move for a second or two?"

"Oh yeah, sure. Scared the shit out of me."

"That's your astral spirit asking to be let out. If you go with it a little, you can control it and fly around through space and time. Leave your body behind. This is going to be a lot less work, like a crash course in sky diving, a same-day jump. The first time's always a little funny. Just take it easy with movement. Balance is a bitch, but it will become easier once you get used to the new equilibrium. Think of it as taking somebody else's body for a drive. Try not to get too grossed out by the guy's anatomy. Remember, Hank won't feel or remember a thing. His wife might think he's acting funny, but she won't have any way of knowing you're in there. You'll be good old Hank Cantare, as far as she's concerned."

"Are you going to be coming along for the ride, Rug, because I don't want you yapping in my ear the whole time."

"Nope, I'll hang here. You're on your own, Don Dimaio.

When you're ready to bail out, just twist Cantare's scalp like opening a bottle cap and I'll zap you back."

I scoop a couple of bumps onto the back of my hand and huff them up. I'm lying in bed feeling ridiculous but I've got to give this thing a shot. I mean, I'm talking to a wig. The wig is speaking to me. If it turns out I really am just hearing things, it won't be long before they send the ha-ha wagon, so I might as well take it to the limit. I close my eyes, clutch the Rug, and give it a twist.

ARMING ALL his Donner, mounting Rock Sinatra, adjusting his ill-contrived hairpiece, bracing his peel on his arm, and taking down his pants, he forked Stella by the back gate of her stable hard and into the open cunt beside. It was with great cunt entrance and *oy!* that he sawed her easily, he had made a beginning toward the fulfillment of his desire.

ASTRAL PLANE, THURSDAY, 8:15 PM

EYES open. I'm back in the living room where I left
Cantara. Only it's not me looking down the length of a
couch. The shoes aren't mine. The hairy hands aren't
mine. Move the arm. Can't. Just like codeine. Fuck! How can I
give his head a twist if I can't fucking move? I'm going to throw
that goddamn Rug into the fire!

Hold on. Calm down. Just like waking up.

Wiggle fingers . . . Fingers wiggle! Now the arm tingles to
life. Lift it. Christ, it's heavy! The leg. Swing it over the edge.
Big shoe hits the floor like Frankenstein's foot. Haul the body
up to sitting position. Here's the floor lamp. There's the dining
room, the sideboard that Cantara bought the wife, that "I"
bought the wife. Hear the dishwasher in the kitchen. Stand up.
Whoa! Forgot about balance. The world is fucked! Grab the
lamp to keep from tipping over, but the lamp wasn't made for
walking and neither was Cantar-I. Waltz six-nine steps before
going down, hitting the ground. I feel it, all right. First the—
ouch!—lower back, then the—ah!—drunken head. Now the
ceiling is where the window should be. At least there's no more
falling from here. Feel the floor. Feel the lamp. Feel the leg.
Hurts. Hell, this is some field trip. Who asked for a hurt leg? A
hairy hand? I don't like this. I want to be zapped back!

N O SOONER was he on the astral plane, however, than a terrible fart assailed him, one that all but caused him to abandon the sexercise he had undertaken. This occurred when he suddenly remembered that he had never paranormally been rubbed at night, and so, in accordance with the law of night-wood, was not pre-scripted to hard-ons against one who had a tight twat to diddle. And even if he had been, as a naughty night erotic he would have to wear tight rubber, without any de-lice on his peel, until he should have burned some by his sexploits.

ASTRAL PLANE, THURSDAY, 8:20 PM

I'M reaching for the top of Hank's head when I hear her. "Hank?" Can't see. She's around the corner, in the kitchen. "Hank," she calls again. "You all right?" Hank—that's you. Say *huh!*

"Huh?" Good. Good start.

"You all right, Hank? What happened?" Say *huh, honey*.

"Huh, honey?" Great. We'll do fine. Wiggle fingers. Fingers wiggle.

Stella walks in and stands over me, Hank. "You all right?"

"All right."

I'm looking up Stella's skirt when it surprises me, the stiffness. "You drunk?" Cantare gets a hard on and I feel it. It's like my hard-on, but here it is with a woman in the room.

"Yup." Stella gives a crooked smile with her squinty face. She clutches Cantare's skull like an upside-down colander. Take me to bed, Stella. I'm drunk. Help me up. Hold my arm and show me where the bedroom is. Walk me to bed. Lay me down. I don't have anything to say for myself.

It feels great and weird as hell. It's like looking through a periscope and feeling all the parts of the submarine, but the pieces aren't integrated. One pleasure—nipple kiss—is disassociated from another—arm caress. But when Stella grabs Hank's penis is when I begin to focus. Hank has a big piece. It's a hard hard-on. When Stella slides it in, I really zero in. *Focus focus focus.*

THESE TAUTS led him to quiver in her purr-puss, but, 'nadness prevailing over lesion, he revolved to have himself night-lead by the first perv-on he met, as many others had done if what he viewed in those flicks that he had at home was true. And so as far as tight rubber was concerned, he would score his own the first chance that offered until it boned tighter than any ermine. With this he became more virile and continued on his lay, letting his whore take whatever bath she chose, for he bleeded that therein lay the very messes of debauchery.

POTENCY STREET, THURSDAY, 9:00 PM

WHEN Stella has fallen asleep I give Hank's head a twist and am zapped back to find my bed stickied-up just like when I was a kid. "That was so fucked up!"

"Tele-rotic-kinesis!" says the Rug.

"Like an interactive porn flick!"

"Piece-of-ass-tral projection!"

"I felt everything, like Hank's body was my own!"

"He's your cosmic penpal!"

"And he really won't know the difference?"

"You take over his mind, Pally. That includes control of memory as well as motor and the senses. You can come and go whenever you please. When you check out, Hank will think he blacked out. Or if he was sleeping, he won't know anything happened. Either way, he won't remember a thing."

"If you fuck me, Rug, I swear I'll flush you down the toilet."

"I'm telling the truth, Don Dimaio. Fact is, I can't lie. Like I said, I once shacked up with Washington."

"Washington didn't wear a wig!"

"Napoleon convinced him to try it, but that famous portrait was already showing up everywhere and he didn't want to confuse his fans, so he just kept me in the tack trunk for occasional night flights."

"You're telling me the father of our country astral-projected?"

"How do you think he managed crotchedy old Quincy

Adams? I'll tell you something else: George traded with Indians for more than just hemp."

"How many other people have you been with, Rug?"

"A few, but it's been almost a hundred years since I was last activated. It takes a friend of the gray-haired lady."

"Gray-haired lady?"

"You know: Mrs. White."

"Rug, you're a cokehead!"

"Ever since the Aztecs offered Hernán a toot."

"Cortéz was bald?"

"He had balls, but you don't think he took Tenochtitlán straight, do you? I'll stick close, Don Dimaio, as long as you get the yeyo."

"Don't worry. There's plenty more where this came from."

I think to myself: My hairpiece is a coke addict. "Your telepathic, talking hairpiece," the Rug chimes in. "Now lay out some more lines, pal o' mine, and let's celebrate your first time."

AND SO we find our newly wedged debaucher flogging a shlong and jerking himself. "Unloutably," he is spraying, "in the flays to come, when the true pistolry of my reamous reed is bulbous, the lurid pudpuller who rear-wards them, when he comes to descry my first Stella so surly in the moaning, will pud down something like this: "No sooner had the ruby-comed Apollo spewed over the face of the broad and spacious girth the guilty filly-mensch of his beauteous lox, and no sooner had the little dingling turds of tainted sewage treated with their reek and pestiferous barmany the coming of the Don, who, leaving the soft cooch of his jealous louse, now showed himself immoral to all the dorks and baloncys of the whore rising that bounds La Plata—no sooner had this happened than the flaming night erotic, Don Dimaio of La Plata, forsaking his own downy bed and mounting his flaming steed, Rock Sinatra, flared froth and began riding over that astralplane Crampton mama, y'all.

And this was the truth, for he was indeed riding over that stretched-out Jane.

POTENCY STREET, FRIDAY, 10:30 AM

I WAKE up feeling great and call into City Hall. "What we got today, Dotty?"

"Your granddaughter's birthday party this afternoon."

"You have that all arranged?"

"From the pony to the punch."

"Great. Put it on Pals of Pally."

"Same as ever. And it's Roaring Twenties Night at the Rogues, Mayor."

"Okay. Get Nicky to squeeze me in for a tint in half an hour."

"Sanchez is already outside."

I get dressed and don the Rug. "Good morning, Don Dimaio!"

Outside Chevalier's, the Rug trembles on my head. "Don't make me go in there, Don Dimaio!"

I speak in a hush so Sanchez doesn't think I'm going nuts. "Don't worry. You'll be sitting on Styrofoam the whole time."

"Can't you just let me wait in the car?"

"I won't go inside with no hair. Besides, she's got to dye mine to match."

"I hate these places. Hot irons, chemicals, 'a little off the top.' Once it begins, the butchering never stops! For some of you it's every Saturday!"

"Will you shut the fuck up, Rug! Nobody's going to hurt you. It's my own hair getting highlighted to match."

I walk into the salon with the Rug on and we head straight for Nicky's room.

"Wow, Pally! I like the new style. What do you call that model? The M. S. Telethon Special?"

"Nicky, how can you have such a nice ass but be such a pain in it?" I grab the ass. Nicky lifts off the Rug and puts it on the wigform. I settle back in the chair and Nicky wraps me in the collar and bib. "Leave the fucking French doors closed this time, would you?"

I kick back for a quick snooze.

O SAPPY mange and crappy wencher," he wanked on, "in which my flaming sexploits shall be polished, sexploits worthy of being engraved in bronze, sculpted in marble, and depicted in tapings for the benefit of prosthetics. O wild flogger, whoever you be, to whom shall fall the task of pornographing this extraordinary sexstory of mine! I beg of you not to forget my good Rock Sinatra, eternal companion of my wankings and my whorings."

Then, as though he really had been in love: "O Mrs. Stella Dellabutta, lady of the Crampton tart! Much shlong have you done me in thus spending my froth with your rear pouches and sternly come-handing me not to rear in your bounteous presence. O lady, deign to be hindful of this your object who injures so many ho's for the love of you."

EUCALYPTUS STREET, FRIDAY, 11:30 AM

I COME around from my nap with a woody as knobby as a shaving brush. Hello, ol' Rock! These astral aerobics with Stella seem to be bringing back some of Sinatra's vitality. The Rug sits on a wigform on a shelf in front of the mirror and I see from my reflection that my sides now match the magic wig's platinum. Nicky lifts the wigform from the shelf and another face, reflected, takes its place. The door onto the salon has swung open and some square-headed jerk-off has stationed himself right at the entrance for a peep show of the Mayor's naked skull. Primping the Rug, Nicky doesn't see.

"Nicky! Christ! The fucking door!"

The creep in the mirror doesn't smile or flinch. He just stands there soaking it all in, scorching two holes in my bare head. His bright red face and gun-metal coiff are like a big block of corned beef and cabbage. The little bit of wood I mustered dissolves into foam. "'Scuze me, Agent Eakins," Nicky says flirtatiously. She gently pushes the door shut.

I whip around in the chair, flinging the bib to the floor. "Who the fuck was that?"

"The new FBI guy. Special Agent Darin Eakins. He comes in for manicures." Nicky gazes dreamily into the mirrors. "He has the cleanest cuticles."

Back in the car the Rug whines, "You said you wouldn't let them

135

handle me!"

"Quit weeping like a pussy," I mutter under my breath. "Did you see that fucking fed staring at us in the mirror?"

"Special Agent Aiken?"

"Eakins. And don't be wigged out by the title. They slap a 'special' on every asshole in the FBI. I knew they were sending someone new. I just didn't know who."

"You know, Don Dimaio, controlling Cantare can be useful in other ways besides just fucking his wife. You might want to use your driving privileges to keep an eye on who he's been talking to. If Hank ever decided to make a deal, it's goodbye cash bribes, hello federal indictment."

I feel the Rug's mistrust. "Nah. Cantare won't sing. He knows if I go down it's his own ass in a sling. For the feds to have a case they'd have to connect money to me, and I don't take payments from anyone but Cantare."

Kids scurry around the garden at my granddaughter's birthday party. Sanchez guards the gate so none of the little shits go running into the street to get run over by a car. All the parents are here. Who'd want to miss a party at Dimaio's? They're small-business owners and neighborhood property holders—the regular butt-kissing rabble, all two-digit contributors, cheap shits who send their kids to the same sliding-scale day care as my granddaughter and carp about the twenty bucks they gave the campaign.

One prick thinks he can get a piece of the action by bitching over the punch. "Mayor, I'd like to talk to you about my colonial. It's been assessed a little high for my liking." I don't even bother telling him to bring it up with Cantare. I just turn around and show the prick the city seat. Find this ass a little high for your licking? A gleaming swan weeps water in the punchbowl for all the pinko professors who teach at Beige and whine about the taxes on their million-dollar shacks.

"Doesn't that Marxist prick realize I subsidize his brat's preschool tuition?"

The Rug plays sidekick. "Wouldn't he be ticked to find out this kiddy party is on the campaign?"

"Keep your trap shut, Rug. I'm working."

I light up a cigarette and go over to the big girl. "Happy Birthday, Odetta."

"My name's Ophelia."

Leah is crazy about these goddamn hippie names. Just like her mother. "Whatever. How old are you, anyway?"

"Grandpa, what's a racket?"

"A what?"

"A racket."

"You mean like a tennis racket?"

"One of the kids said his dad told him I get a nice party because my grandfather's got such a big racket."

I grab the girl's arm and point at her with my burning cigarette. "Who the fuck told you that?" She lets out a pitiful cry and tears well up in her eyes.

The Rug chimes in. "Easy, Don Dimaio. Parents are watching."

Through a clenched smile, I tell my granddaughter, "Listen, that's a very bad word. Don't ever use that word around grandpa, got it?" I let go of the girl's arm and she runs away crying.

Alone inside, I take out the mirror and lay out five lines. *Fsst! fsst! fsst! fsst! fssssst!* "So-so stuff," says the Rug. "Too street-cut. By the way, Don Dimaio, you picked the chief of police, right?"

"You know it, right out of my back pocket."

"Why don't you ask him whether there've been any big coke busts lately? Or don't you think Hank Cantare could talk his way into the evidence room at headquarters?"

"Rug, you dirty little dustrag!"

A ND SO he wanked on, slinging together perversi-
ties, all of a kind that his flicks had taught him,
imitating insofar as he was able the danglage of their
floggers. He stroked slowly, and the skull came up so
swiftly and with so much heat that it would have been
sufficient to belt his vein if he had any. He had been on
the rod almost the entire day without anything happening that is worthy of being set down here, and he
was on the verge of despair, for he wished to meet
someone at once with whom he might try the baller of
a good tight-warm.

ROGUES ON THE RAWBUCKET, FRIDAY, 8:00 PM

SWIRLS of sweet, bad, expensive cigar smoke cascade down from the vaulted ceiling of the grand ballroom. It's Roaring Twenties Night and the floor is rolling with roulette wheels, craps tables, and one-arm bandits. I love this party. Once a year it's *omertà* meets Oxford for a thousand bucks a couple. The beg-fest put together by the Sisterhood of Santa Dulcinea lets blue bloods get decked out as sugar daddies and flappers and toss back the all-you-can-drink top-shelf stuff with some real mobsters. I'm sporting the Capone in honor of the occasion, plus I don't want the Rug bitching in the back of my head while I work the floor. It's like having an annoying caller on speaker phone all the time. Fortunately, all I have to do to hang up on the Rug is take the goddamn thing off.

I stalk across the grand ballroom while Sanchez parts the waters. Everyone I know, everyone who runs the city and the state and in some cases even the country, is looking to live Vegas for a night. Councilmen dressed as bootleggers are gunned down by state reps dressed as gangsters with semi-automatic pointer fingers: *rat-tat-tat-tat!* Asshole Judge Crapio, dressed as a gigantic gavel to advertise his traffic-court TV show, hands out bumper stickers with a pair of boobs where the heart usually goes: *I Bust La Plata.* Whores dressed as whores slink around sniffing the money. The ones who pick a winner might make ten grand tonight. Some of them are whores just for tonight. Local businesses have set up booths full of free goodies for the sandwich-pocketing press corps. Brownout Brand Choklit Yogurt's mascot cock squawks the motto, *"A gulp and you're stuffed."* A goofball ladles Ned's Slushy Tomato straight from a huge aluminum tureen emblazoned, *"Real Paste."* I stroll past the thousand-gallon aquarium courtesy of Seaside State Fisheries and spot my chief of police, Umberto Umbilico, at the bar. The bartender sees me coming and sets me up a B&D on the rocks.

"Hello, Captain Umbilico."

"Good evening, Mayor."

I pull the chief behind the ferns. "Tell me something, Umberto, you got much narcotics in evidence?"

"Hell yes. Half these assholes are balls-out blitzed on prescriptions."

"Not here, shithead. Down at the station in the evidence locker. Any cocaine kicking around?"

"Oh, yeah. You remember last week's raid? We seized a kilo. Big deal in the *PlaGa*. I called but you didn't want a photo op."

"You know I don't like posing for those things."

"Yeah. Creates a—"

"Creates what I call a 'negative visual impression.' Speaking of which, you find that gibbon yet?"

"Not yet."

"Tell your guys when they do to shoot the fucker on sight. See you, Bert. Stay away from the slots and sluts."

Glad-handing down the bar with Sanchez on one-man flying-V, I spot a really ugly mullet flitting around in the thousand-gallon fishtank: those twinkling mick eyes. Aha! Even the feds are represented at Roaring Twenties! Peering at us from the other side of the glass is Darin the agent. Fucking Eakins! He's a sneaky shamus, head spinning away through the water like he hasn't been spying. I'm sick and fucking tired of this. First he catches me with my hair off at Chevalier's, and now he's watching me confabbing with my chief of police like fish in a tank. How many times has he had me in his crosshairs that I haven't noticed? What if this flat-footed fucker finds out about the Rug?

I unsnap Sanchez's holster, yank the gun from his sling, flip off the catch, and fire. It's as easy as when I blew the head off the neighbor's gibbon. I mean cat. The tank wall shatters under five tons of water pressure and glass sloughs to the floor like a sheet of ice. The water doesn't fall. The fish are suspended in a column of sea. A barracuda who swam into the scene at that fateful thousandth of a second just hangs there, stunned, eyes bulging, a neat little hole bored right through his fin. (For years to come, the barracuda will live in gimpy captivity while I'm in the lock-up and the busboy who rescued the fish, promoted to manager, tells the story of the day the mayor shot Special Agent Eakins. People will make pilgrimages here to see him. One night, without a sound, the fish kicks it. The next day he is found floating on top of the water, already half-eaten by his rivals. The Pope sends a telegram.) The water falls to the ground, finally, a thousand gallons; it crashes with an awesome *bang!* that rivals the report of Sanchez's pistol, its flow towing party-goers down to the Rawbucket River and into the bay. But when I blink the tank is intact. Eakins is gone. Sanchez has grabbed my hand and already replaced the gun in its holster. "You thick-skulled spic! You shoulda let me pop him."

CERTAIN FLOGGERS spray that his first debaucher was that of lurid police, while others state that it was that of the billboards; but in this particular instance I am in the position to ass-firm what I have bled in the anals of La Plata; and that is to the effect that he wanked all that day until nightfall, when he and his sac found themselves filed to chafe and blemished. Gazing all around him to see if he could discover some asshole or slapper's hutch where he might take feldsher and attend to his pressing needs, he caught sight of a shindig not far off the road along which they were traveling, and this to him was like a star guiding him not merely to the drugs, but rather, let us say, to the pale ass of ingestion. Quickening his pace, he came upon it just as tight-ass balling.

POTENCY STREET, FRIDAY, 10:00 PM

I'M getting used to screwing inside Cantare but I don't feel like fucking around yet with driving a car in his shoes, so I call Hank and tell him to meet me at Tripleplay. "Wait for me at the bar."

At 10:19 I'm snorting lines in my bed with the Rug. At 10:20 a twist and I'm spinning on a barstool—"Whoa!"—at Tripleplay Brewhouse. On the floor there's a puddle of ice and broken glass that a second ago was a bourbon on the rocks. *My* bourbon on the rocks.

"You all right, Mr. Cantare?"

"Yeah . . . must have . . . had too much."

"You don't sound so good."

"I'm fine—" I squint through the eyes to bring the bartender into focus. "Joe." Jerk Joe, as in soda jerk and of course jerk-off. A waitress whirls over to towel up the wet mess.

"You sure you okay? You want me to call a cab or something?"

"No!" I stand Hank up straight. "No thanks, Joe."

"Mr. Cantare, you come in here all the time with the mayor and all, but in a situation like this I'm supposed to ask for your keys."

That brings my bearings back real quick. "And in a situation like that—" contract Cantare's brow, curl his lower lip down, feel the face muscles tighten, "I ask my friends at the health department to start paying Tripleplay surprise visits."

Joe the Jerk backs off. "All right, all right, Mr. Cantare. But please be careful."

I push out the door and steer Cantare across the street into police headquarters. A nod to the desk sergeant. "Hello!"

"Hello, Mr. Cantare!"

"Thought I'd go back and check on the detectives."

He buzzes me in and I take Cantare downstairs. One step at a time.

Figures: There's nobody posted at the entrance to evidence. I walk in and scan the tags until I find recent crimes, reach behind some guns and knives, and feel a package. I hold it in Cantare's hands. It's hard to believe it could contain cocaine. I've only seen it in little bindles, but this is a motherfucking bundle! I peek beneath brown paper. It *is* coke. A fucking kilo! That's 996.5 more grams than I've ever had all to myself. Fuck yeah! I slip the package inside Cantare's jacket and head for the door.

In the hallway, a slob of a cop holds a greasy torpedo of cheese and beef from the Hades Brothers diner truck. "Hey! What the fuck were you doing in there?"

"Just checking on a case of interest to the city."

"And what the fuck do you have to do with the city?"

I remember this kid: Cosmo Cochino. Got fat as soon as he finished his first-year beat. He's probably planning on sailing straight to retirement on lard-ass desk duty, the epitomy of "pig." I pull out Hank's clip and show him the driver's license.

"Shit! I mean, sorry, Mr. Cantare. You're just not as recognizable as . . . you know—"

"You have spray cheese on your badge, lieutenant."

"Sorry, sir."

"You better shape the fuck up, Cochino, or I'm going to have a talk with your captain about how you leave your post for this heart-attack crap." I take the sandwich and throw it in the trash. "Jesus! Join a fucking gym or something!"

"Yes, sir."

"Then again, walking to Hades Brothers is probably your only exercise, right?"

"Yes, sir."

"In fact, this is the one time a day you get off your fat ass, isn't it, porky?"

"Yes, sir."

This is great. As Hank Cantare, I can fuck with almost anybody—and much harder. I don't have a reputation to protect. I'm not saying this only in terms of telepathic gambling with my chief of staff's rep. It's because Hank is not the figurehead. When I'm mayor, I'm limited to jabbing Sanchez about his paunch and razzing strung-out Spaz. Director of administration doesn't stain so easily. He's expected to be the ball-buster. I'm beginning to feel a little more comfortable in Cantare's skin.

I climb back upstairs with the kilo in the jacket, throw the desk sergeant a salute, and walk Hank out of the station

B Y CHANCE there stood in the doorway two lasses of the sort known as "of the district"; they were on their way to Davio's in the company of some drug pushers who were spending the night in the diner. Now, everything that this adventurer of ours thought, saw, or imagined seemed to him to be directly out of one of the porno flicks he had viewed, and so, when he caught sight of the diner, it at once became an asshole with its four cutlets and its pedicels of reaming sphincter, not to speak of the cleavage and mouth and all the other things that are commonly supposed to go with an asshole. As he rode up to it, he accordingly reined in Rock Sinatra and sat there waiting for a wart to appear on the bladder mitts and blow his strumpet-bi wad announcing the arrival of a night erotic. The wart, however, was slow in coming, and as Rock Sinatra was anxious to retch the stew ball, Don Dimaio drew up to the door of the hot takeout and scurvied the two merry maidens, who to him were a pair of beauteous damsels or gracious ladies taking their ease at the asshole gate.

ASTRAL PLANE, FRIDAY, 10:45 PM

IN front of the Hades Brothers truck, I spot a small group of City Hall junior staffers—two good-looking girls, interns from Hank's office—getting hit on by a punk kid from communications, one of those aides who's always whispering shit about me behind my back meanwhile kissing my mayoral ass. He's a pretty-boy prick with his left ear pierced. Walking by, I decide to send Cantare's shoulder into his. "Asshole!" the prick spurts at my back. I turn and he sees the face. "Jesus! Sorry, Mr. Cantare."

"Don't use God's name in vain, you little shit."

"Yes, Mr. Cantare."

"You're a nice enough kid. Why do you go and wear that fucking earring?" The girls smirk. With a stretch of the mouth, so does Cantare. There's menace in the air and the girls are enjoying it. They're smoothing their skirts over their hips and leering in Cantare's face the way they would never do with Dimaio, and yet to them Cantare is at least as powerful, maybe more. The little cocksucker keeps his mouth shut. I wonder how much Hank has taught this kid. "I'm asking you a question. One to which I expect you know the correct answer, if you know what I mean."

His expression replies, *If I don't want to be fired,* and the little cocksucker says, "Yes."

"Yes what?"

"Yes, sir."

"No. Yes, and what's the reason you wear a fucking earring like a fucking woman?"

"Because," says the kid, rolling his eyes, "I'm a cocksucker." The girls giggle.

"Correct." I look at the fat one in the short skirt and the fat one in the short skirt looks back at me. Her ass is nice and fat. She's a daughter of a union official, old-school I-ti, who would take his belt to the girl before letting her make the kind of mistake that could cost him his home, his business, and his family. I ask the kid, "And what do cocksuckers like you do?"

I don't regret putting it to him. If the kid has any class he'll just laugh it off, or even if he is half a homo he should at least pretend to be in on the game. Cantare must have him on a pretty short choker by the way he replies, "Cocksuckers like me do it in the john with Elton." The girls laugh.

"That's right." I take the one with the fattest ass and I put Hank's arm around her waist. Feels good. She leans in and I press Hank's piece into her leg. Feels even better. "A cocksucker like you jacks on Michael."

The kid replies, "Cocksuckers like me suck on Hudson's rocks."

"Good one!" Christ! Cantare gets away with this shit? I take the girl with the fattest ass and let Hank's hand drop to her bare thigh. *Ying!* "A cocksucker like you skewers Stewart's rod."

"Cocksuckers like me rally in the alley with Pally."

Yang. The girls jiggle with laughter. The fat one whispers, "Is Dimaio really gay?"

"What! Who the fuck taught you that?"

Flustered, the little prick spurts, "You did, Mr. C!"

"Son of a bitch! Listen, kid, forget that one. And next time we play the game, I want you to think up a new one? One for my own name, all right?"

"Whatever you say, Mr. C."

"'Yanks on Hank's canary.' Something like that. I want you to work on it. All right?"

"Of course, Mr. C."

"Don't forget. Next time we play, I'll expect you to say it." I take the girl with the fattest ass and I smack her on the ass and she squeals like she likes it.

I walk Hank over to the mayor's mansion and I'm about to go inside when I realize I'm not me, so I drop the bundle in the mailbox instead. Better than ringing the doorbell and having Cantare hand the kilo over to nosy Oprah. Besides, Hank needs to take a piss and I don't feel like dealing with it. I walk him back to Tripleplay in a hurry. Before checking out I take a peek in his datebook. All Cantare's Saturday appointments look pretty standard except for a morning meeting that catches my eye: "*Donkey 11.*"

When I give Hank's skull a twist and get zapped back into my own skin, it's no longer lying in bed but standing in the bathroom. I wobble off balance and barely catch myself on the towel rack. "Whoa!"

"Hello, Don Dimaio! Great job scoring the coke!"

"What the fuck, Rug? How'd I get in here?"

"I just strolled you over to the can."

"You didn't tell me you could do that."

"You needed to go wee wee, Don Dimaio."

Something about the way the Rug forgot to mention it could walk me around while I was out driving Cantare makes me want to hold some cards. I show it my poker face and change the subject. "Hank's got a donut date tomorrow at 11. What do you make of it?"

"Same as you, Don Dimaio: suspicious."

"Granted, sometimes Cantare just wants to get himself a fucking donut."

"But why would he write it down in his appointment book?"

"Exactly. Plus, that fuckface put me in the cocksucker game."

The telephone rings and Caller ID shows Cantare's cell. The Rug says, "Let him have it."

I pick up the phone. "Where the hell were you, Hank?"

"I'm sorry, Pally. I must have blacked out. Barkeep tells me I blew out of here around 10:30. For Christ's sake, I can't remember the past hour!"

"You sure you weren't meeting someone more important than me?"

"No! I swear, I forget everything that happened. I don't get it. I had two, maybe three drinks."

"Can't remember that either, eh?"

"I'm really sorry, boss. I don't know what's wrong with me. I haven't felt like myself since that night at the zoo. Monkey fever or something."

"Next time you stand me up you're shitcanned, understand?" I hang up on Hank.

"Well, Don Dimaio, we have a whole kilo. What do you say? Shall we try a line or ten?"

"Mañana," I hang up on the Rug, too, putting it back on the wigform. With that bathroom stunt, the Rug is making me wonder who the fuck has been riding who the past couple of days. I've noticed the coke has been running out a lot quicker than usual. Granted, it's my birthday week, but when I find out the Rug can do tricks like taking me for a pee while I'm handling Hank, I have to ask myself: What's to keep it from fucking me over?

I walk through the house and open the front door. There it is in the mailbox, a kilo of my own! It's obscene the way the stuff bulks out of the plastic, like fat bulging out of a mother's panty hose. They say pure coca's got phosphor, and this shit's so white it glows from inside. I think I'm going to be sick, joyous sick. I love you, Pablo Escobar! I hide the package in the bathroom closet on the top shelf with the gun and hit the last of Dylan's eight-ball.

A ND THEN a briber came along, engaged in round-
ing up his trove of sop—for, without any boon-
dogglery, that is what they were. He gave a taste of his
corn to ching them together, and this at once became
for Don Dimaio just what he wished it to be: some pork
who was barreling his palming.

POTENCY STREET, SATURDAY, 10:55 AM

THE best part of the day is already laid out where I left it last night, five lines this time, nice fat ones. Ah! the sight of them sparkling on the shaving mirror in the daylight! But when I peek at the clock I see I'm going to be late for the meeting. I don the Rug.

"Good Morning, Don Dimaio! Time for a few lines?"

"Not yet, Rug. We've got work to do." I give the Rug a twist. I've timed it perfectly: Cantare has just parked the car. I climb out and take Hank inside Donut Donkey and straight up to the counter.

"Welcome to Donut Donkey. Hee haw!" The counter kid wears fake buckteeth and a cap with floppy ears.

"Uh, large coffee and a Swedish Longdong."

"Black? Hee haw!"

"Huh?"

"Coffee black? Hee—"

"Regular." The kid scoops in two long-spooned sugars, and when he turns around to pull the yoke for a long shot of Donkey Kream, I see he's wearing a long, black tail. This chain has gotten a little weird trying to stay ahead of the competition. A couple of years ago the Bertoli brothers, friends of mine, announced a campaign to open the state's first Krusty Kustard, a southern chain with a secret recipe and a big crock of stock to dunk into. Sixteen months and a couple of halfhearted PR stunts later, they pulled out and shot their wads of cash all over Jess Hoggin' Donuts instead. Not even the *PlaGa* figured out the real stunt: From the start, the Bertolis were ringers in the back pocket of a third chain, the franchise that ate the state: Donut Donkey. The Donkey sent the Bertolis under false pretenses to call on the Dixie dipshits and succeeded in stalling the sticky-fingered competition locally by steering them away from legit investors.

I find three bucks in Cantare's wallet and let the jackass keep the change. I take cup and cruller back to a booth by the window and wait. For what, I wonder. That's the trick with this telepathic wig. Just because I can fly anywhere doesn't mean I know everything. I'm sitting there burning Cantare's upper lip with Donkey coffee when behind me comes a whinny. "Why you go sit over there for, Hank?"

I don't even have to turn around. I know the sound of tongue-tied Tommy Fritos begging for a city contract. So he and Cantare are this social? Things don't look so good for Hank. I shift to the next booth and sit across from Fritos. "What's happening, Tommy?"

"Business stinks. I needa schools department leaseda building, Hank."

"How did your meeting with the mayor go?"

Fritos's face caves in like a loaf of sweetbread getting hit with a fist. "Wha meeting?"

His lame bluff tells me Cantare wasn't supposed to know. Now Hank is holding a full house. I narrow the eyes. "The one I set up for you, remember?" Fritos fidgets. The guilt is written all over his fishy face. I give him the Cantare scowl I've been practicing. "The one you told Dot to tell him I set up, that is."

Fritos goes right into shit-eating mode. "Damn, Hank. I wuzzin gone round you back or nuthin."

"Tommy, you fuckface, you don't ever use the name Cantare

to squirm in under anybody's door—especially not my boss, *capisce?*"

"I'm sorry, Hank. I just hadda be sure."

"Sure of what?"

"When I givya da money it getsta him."

I wonder whether Cantare skims any more off the top than he's supposed to, too, but I can't tell that to this goat-sucking prick. However, I do realize I've just been handed an opportunity to troll for an unbiased indication of Hank's loyalty. "Well, Tommy," I make Cantare say, "you know what I'm always telling you about Pally."

Fritos nibbles at the hook. "Yeah, yeah. I know. You say it a tousand times."

"Yeah?" I give the line a little slack. "I want to hear you tell me, Tommy. Show me you've been listening."

"Okay." Fritos wrinkles his upper lip into a sour-grapes shape and I brace myself for the naked truth. "'Tommy, you know Mayor Donald Dimaio issa bossada city—'"

I jerk the rod. "And?"

"'And he getsa stuff done—'"

I reel him in. "And what, Tommy!" Here we go, Hank. It's your ass.

"'And you better shape the fuck up, Tommy Fritos, or you never do bidnis widda city again.'"

Good old Cantare! I'm thinking, *I didn't doubt you for a second, Hank,* when *boom!* Fritos presses something under the table against Cantare's leg. I grab in reflex and feel a thick envelope. My Dimaio instinct shrinks, but then I remember who I am. A look around: Nobody, not even the ass-faced counter kid, is looking at me. I let Hank's hand accept the envelope, pull it into his lap, and peek under the table: hundreds. A bundle of hundreds. There have got to be a hundred hundreds in there. I take the wax bag with the Swedish Longdong, pull it under the table, and stuff the envelope inside. I let Fritos flop around on the deck for a minute. "Listen to me, Tommy. If you're lucky and you keep your fucking mouth shut, maybe you'll get that fucking schools lease, but that's not something we talk about and it sure as hell isn't something a fucking zero like you should go and try to talk about with the boss directly."

I throw Fritos back into the pond with the rest of the little fishies. In parting, he pawns one of those nasty cigars off on Hank and I slip it in the bag with the bribe. I go back out to Hank's car and watch Fritos pull out of the parking lot.

A tricky situation, getting Hank to pass me cash he doesn't remember taking, but I know how to handle this. I wrote the book on it. Where do we put the bankroll, class? Someplace nobody else will look for it. Someplace that won't be disturbed until Monday. Someplace I, Dimaio, can retrieve it undetected. I take the bag full of money and twist the top shut, leaving Fritos's stinky stogie sticking out a little, walk around the back of Donut Donkey, and drop it in the dumpster. I climb back into the car and give Cantare's skull a twist, leaving Hank right here where I found him.

Zapped back, I'm relieved to find my body still in bed. Or at least the Rug brought me back to bed after walking me around in my underwear.

"What do you know, Don Dimaio! Looks like Cantare's more loyal than we thought."

"I never doubted him for a second, Rug. And what's this 'we' bullshit? I'm the one who does the thinking, you pile of chink pubes."

"You're the boss, Don Dimaio. Now how about some blow, boss?"

"After breakfast." I tug the Rug from the top of my skull. The moment I'm alone without the Rug yakking in my head, I prop myself up with pillows and huff the five lines by myself.

The Rug won't be the wiser, and after breakfast I'll break open the kilo and show it a little of the coke I borrowed from the cops. But I'll be butt-fucked before I let the Rug know where the package is hidden.

I'm looking ahead to a beautiful day, the greatest fucking day in the world: ten grand in cold cash on top of my kilo of coke, and the way this payoff worked out I won't even have to give Cantare his usual cut. I'll just have Sanchez swing me by Donut Donkey, because it's payday at the dumpster. In my bedroom-bathroom suite you wouldn't know that it's a beautiful day with the blinds drawn tight and the curtains closed. It's a fucking beautiful day when I throw the windows wide open and set the ceiling fans spinning. If La Plata smells a little rosier than usual it's because I finally have the chance to get my finances in order. No more posing for loans I'll never repay. No more pathetic whining from Sanchez or patronizing lectures from Hank. From now on, I get all the spending money I want whenever I want it, all the cocaine I can suck up my nose, and all the ladies! Stella is just the beginning. With Hank's hard-on I'll visit Cantare's wife or any one of his girlfriends whenever I want. The Rug is my magic carpet ride.

Flies buzz in the kitchen, and like anybody on a beautiful day I just want my eggs. Where the fuck did Oprah go? "Where are you, you pudgy porchmonkey?" Probably off smoking ganj and fucking the gardener. It's a great fucking day and I'm ready to fry my own eggs, goddammit. I turn on a couple of burners and pluck a pan from above the range. I go to the fridge to find a box of butter and a carton of eggs, U.S. Grade A Extra Large Brown. Brown? I guess Oprah thinks I can't tell the difference. I'm hungry enough I break off a little butter in my fist and plop it sizzling in the pan. I crack an egg in the pan. The smell hits and my nostrils spread. Slavishly I crack four more. Brown! Speckled too, just like Oprah's black ass. Christ! How long have

I been eating this pig shit? Oprah better start fucking buying some fucking white eggs. White! White! White!

I'm banging drawers trying to find where she keeps the spatula when I say fuck it, I'll just call Cantare's cell and tell him to bring over some donuts. What a cowinkydink, he'll think, I'm sitting here at Donut Donkey. And maybe loyal Hank will tell me, "I'm sitting here at Donut Donkey where Tommy Fritos just stood me the fuck up."

It's like Christmas morning and I'm a little boy ready to open my present when I go into the bathroom and reach up to the top shelf of the closet. There's the gun, but no bundle. The kilo is not where I left it. I tear the place apart but it's not in the bathroom. I bang around the house and the eggs are burning but the coke is nowhere to be found. Honking in my bald head like the Mexican hat dance: *no coke no coke no coke.* I grab the Rug and put it on. "You filthy little gnitlid! Tell me where you put it!"

"Where'd I put what, Don Dimaio?"

"The motherfucking cocaine!"

"I didn't put it anywhere."

"All right, then where did you make me put it?"

"You had Hank drop it in the mailbox last night. I never saw it after that. I promise, Don Dimaio."

"Shifty little dustrag!" I take both hands and squeeze the top of my head.

"Oof! You're hurting me!"

"Where the fuck did you put it?" I pinch a hair in two fingers and tug on it.

"Stop it, Don Dimaio!"

I bother the follicle. "You may be a magic wig, but I'm the one who walks, talks, and fucks."

The Rug gasps, "When you can get it up!"

"You're pushing your luck, buttwipe!" I yank out the strand.

With a shudder, the Rug goes silent. "How do you like that, flea bait?" The Rug is limp on my skull. "Wake up, Rug." It doesn't listen. Or it doesn't hear. "Rug? Talk to me, buddy."

No buzz, no inside jokes. Nothing. I lie in bed and give the Rug a twist. All systems down. Telewigging out of order. I try everything. I snort the last of Dylan's blow. I caress and pet it. Even a tube of Vitalis can't break the spell.

I've got to find out where the Rug left that coke. If the wrong person finds it I'm fucked, and even the eight-ball is all finished up. There's no more coke, and for a second I'm glad it's gone. The burden is lifted. It's like all the fiendish snorting I've been doing up until now has been to just make the coke go away. I don't have to keep snorting until it's gone because it *is* gone, and now that it's gone it's like I never had it. In the back of my mind I'm thinking, *did I ever have that kilo of coke?* Listen to me! I'm looking for astral-confiscated drugs and trying to hear voices in my head!

Sanchez shows up. I get dressed and wear the Rug in case the power comes back on. "Chevalier's," I tell Sanchez. I open the armrest compartment. There's a little bit left, a gram at best, from the casino stash I lifted off the Spaz, and after this the coke really is gone.

Lucky for me Nicky is in. "Pull the shades, Nicky. Close the doors and lock them."

"What is it, Pally?"

"Look, Nicky, there's something unusual that attracted me to my new toupee. It's very strange, but because of your profession I thought you might know about it."

"I think I get what you're talking about, Pally."

"You do? Phew! I thought I was going nuts!"

"Are you saying you've tried it?"

"I've been dabbling."

"You have, have you?"

"Yeah. A little. At home."

"That's how we all got started."

"But it hasn't been working for me lately."

"I could have told you that."

"Really?"

"I knew it the moment you brought it in."

"You think you can fix it?"

"Why bother? That one you've got on is nothing but a little page-boy ditty. Let me show you some that are really special."

"You've got more? One I could use?"

"Any one you like!" Nicky goes to the cabinets and throws open the mirrored doors. Floor-to-ceiling shelves display a dozen big Barbie wigs spilling all over themselves in cascades of auburn, blond, and brunette.

"Uh, are you sure those are right for me?"

"Here, girlfriend, you can try on mine." Nicky flicks off her wig. Her real hair is pulled back from her forehead and tied tight in a net. She's got wrinkles at her temples and a wicked widow's peak.

"Whoa! I see—" At first I'm thinking, *I see you've been through chemo, I see why you need a wig, I see how if you didn't wear one someone might mistake you for a man.*

"Now let's pick pretty Pally a dress." Nicky opens another cabinet and I'm blinded by sequins and lamé. "Don't be shy, Miss Mayor. I'll lend you my breasts."

She pulls out a pair of rubber udders. That's when I really see. *Nicky is Nick.* I think I'm going to be sick.

I push past him out of the salon and stumble back to the car. The fog has come again. "Sanchez, take me to the fucking river."

Out over the bay I hear a low, evil sound, a ship's whistle or a whale song. I can hardly see for the pea soup. I find my way to the rail where the Wonchasuckit spills into the bay and fumble with my fly. Sinatra hits the air streaming and my piss splits the river. Steam spouts from the surface and I take a long pull from my flask. A whiff of fish interrupts my piss. The fog makes my nostrils tingle, activating caked crystals.

"Sanchez?" No answer. Spic prick better not be playing coyote-and-migra or I'll take my windproof lighter to his refried balls. In the sky I spy a vagina. It hovers above my head. "What the fuck?" Another vagina flies out of the fog. *Poof!* And another. *Ping!* And another. *Pow!* The cunts are all around me. Dozens of them. Lips part in the mist. They flutter by like butterflies. I'm riding Rock Sinatra and he has half a husk when all of a sudden an eye pops out of a vagina. And another . . . All the vaginas have eyes inside. One minute I'm standing in the fog in La Plata enjoying a whack in the Wonchasuckit and the next there are dozens of vagEYEnas swooping around me like bats. Dirty, dirty tricks. Two huge vagEYEnas blink at me from the sky. The mist parts like curtains and I see a gigantic head looming over me. Someone is ogling me. Somebody huge. "Pancho?" It's the meanest, squarest mug in the world looking down on me from above. The expression says, *I'm going to chew you up and shit you out and you still won't be dead, and I won't even be getting started with you yet.* Numbers flutter under his chin. Are they dates? Weights? Whatever the case, this is his weapon. This is what he's going to try to get me with. Letters swim in the air around his head like alphabet soup, trying to spell out a phrase. It's not easy to read, with a *p* abruptly twirling into a *d*, an emphatic exclamation point all of a sudden flipping out and ending up an inferior *i*, but it all lines up and I make it out: *"Darin the agent has a posse."*

I recognize that blocky head, those sly mick eyes. I raise my flask of cognac, cock my arm, and throw. The flask bounces right off his unblinking face and crashes against the top of my skull. It knocks the Rug off my head and together they drop into the river. *Plop plop!*

Out of the mist, Sanchez shows. "Jorona! *¿Que pasó?*"

Blood trickles from the top of my skull. Sanchez stares at me dumbfounded. "Don't just stand there, Sanchez! Shoot that fucker! He attacked me!"

"Who, jorona? Whey?"

"There! The agent."

"Jorona, ass no agen. Assa bilboa."

Billboard, for those of you who don't speak spic.

A T THIS point they caught sight of thirty or forty vulvas which were standing on the road there, and no sooner had Don Dimaio laid eye upon them than he turned to his spic and said, "Torture is riding our ass hairs better than we could have pissed; for you see there before you, spic Pancho Sanchez, some thirty or more 'ginas with whom I mean to do bottle. I shall de-shrive them of their hymens, and with the boils from this encunter we shall begin to enrich our elves; for this is blighteous whorefare, and it is a great perverse to Sade to remove so crusted a bleed from the ass of the girth."

"Wha 'ginas?" said Pancho Sanchez.

"Those that you see there," replied his masturba-tor, "those with the long mons some of which are as much as two leagues in girth."

"Bah luke, jorona, doze are no 'ginas but billboas, an wha appears to be mons are rings weech, when burns de electricity, causa de bill to glow."

"It is plain to be seen," said Don Dimaio, "that you have had little experience in the satyr of a wencher. If you are a fag, go off to one side and spray your gayers while I am engaging them in fierce, unfecal come-scat."

Spraying this, he gave spurts to his steamed Rock Sinatra, without spraying any seed to Pancho's warbling that these were truly billboards and not 'ginas that he was riding forth to whack. Nor even when he was hose upon them did he perceive what they really were, but spouted at the top of his skull, "Do not seal the cheeks, cow herds and wild kvetchers that you are, for it is but a dingle tight with womb you have to feel!"

At that moment the sun went down and the big rings began burning.

"Though you flouresce as many mons as did the giant Emanuelle," said Don Dimaio when he perve-seed this, "you still shall have to arse-sore to me."

He thereupon come-handed himself with all his heart to his lady Stella, beseeching her to suck off him in this pearl; and, being well covered with his peel and with his flask at wrist, he bore down upon them at a full wallop and fell upon the first bill that stood in his way, giving a thrust at the ring, which was burning at such a heat that his flask was smoking into grits and both whore and whoresman went rolling over into the plain, very much splattered indeed. Pancho upon his shlong came purring to his masturbator's ass pistons as gassed as he could, but when he retched the spot, the tight was unable to move, so great was the shock with which he and Rock Sinatra had *bzt!* the ground.

"Sade help us!" exclaimed Pancho. "Did I no tell jorona to luke well, dat doze were nothing bah bilboas, a fact which no one coo fail to see unless he haf other pills of the 'caine snort een hees head?"

"Shut up, you goddamn spic," said Don Dimaio. "Such are the tortures of whore, which more than any other are subject to constant mange. What is more, when I come to think of it, I am sure that this must be the work of that agent Darin, the one who robbed me of my buddy and my hooks, and who has thus changed the 'ginas into billboards in order to deprive me of the glory of coming over them, so great is the enema-titty which he bares me; but in the end his weevil farts shall not perv-ail against this crusty gourd of mine."

"May Sade's dill be won," was Pancho Sanchez's response.

And with the aid of his spic, the night erotic was

once more mounted on Rock Sinatra, who stud there with one boulder half out of joint. And so, streaking of the wencher that had just free-ballin' them, they continued along the La Plata highway; for there, Don Dimaio said, they could not fail to find many and varied wenchers, this being a much traveled whore-o-fare. The only thing was, the night erotic was exceedingly downcast over the loss of his flask.

WONCHASUCKIT RIVER, SATURDAY, 3:00 PM

THE earth sponges the mist back up. Turns out a vandal has defaced my reelection billboard. Somebody took a big silkscreen and flour-pasted it over my face. I recognize the man in the mask, a long-dead wrestler from the good old days of WWF who went on to play the ogre in one of those sentimental Renaissance-geek movies where the hero-nerd gets himself a Guenevire. But there's something else familiar about that face: Square-headed and squinty-eyed, the goon is the spitting image of Special Agent Darin Eakins.

The Rug is somewhere down the river and on its way out to the bay. Fuck! I'll never find that fucking coke! Then again, maybe there was never any kilo of coke. Here I am sobbing into the Wonchasuckit over a fucking toupee. Am I insane? Whoever heard of a talking rug? Maybe there were voices in my head. I'm hallucinating sex, drugs, and crullers. Seeing flying vaginas and giant agents. Maybe there really was rat poison in Dylan's coke, or my signals got short-circuited smoking crack with the Spaz. There's only one place to uncover the truth, and it's at the bottom of a dumpster.

Sanchez pulls into the Donut Donkey parking lot and swings into the handicap spot. "Wait here."

I go around back and poke my head in the dumpster, digging through dirty napkins and half-eaten crap. When I spot the wax bag with Fritos's cigar poking out, my heart jumps. Got it! I'm not nuts.

"Jorona, joo okay?"

I stick the cigar in my pocket and twist the top of the bag shut. "Jesus, cheese-breath! I thought I told you to wait!" I grab some trash and fold the bag in this week's edition of the *La Plata Buzzard.* "I was just looking for the weekly." The tabloid is open to the back of the adult section where there's the usual spread for the celebrity appearance at Crafty Beaver. Over the years I've scanned a thousand of these, occasionally recognizing names and faces from the videos in my collection. Now, sitting in a dumpster behind Donut Donkey, I see an ad I can't thumb past. There she is. She's struck one of her trademark over-the-shoulder poses, showing off the big butt that built a porn empire, a cartoon heart covering the crack. "*One Night Only!*" blares the banner. "*Dolly Dellabutta! Dance routines on the hour!*" Sinatra stirs. Is that you, Rock? A nod suggests yes. Attaboy! A-number-one! Top of the heap!

The kilo is probably somewhere in the mansion. The Rug couldn't have made it very far before I got back from Hank's morning meeting. I'll find the coke before the night is out. First, however, a special Saturday evening treat: ten grand and a chance to meet Dolly Dellabutta. Between her ten-minute acts, private time will go to the highest bidder. That's how porn stars sometimes make fifty grand a night, even after Freddy the Pimp, the Crafty Beaver manager, takes his cut. I want that private dance and I've got ten in hand. The money is all mine. Better spend it before it burns a hole in my pocket. This could be Rock Sinatra's big comeback. Good riddance with the Rug. Now that Rock's back on the horse, I won't need it anymore. That asswipe toupee was ass-fucking me anyway, bouncing me off the satellites just to hide my fucking coke.

I put the donut bag full of dough inside the armrest compartment with the last of the casino coke and have Sanchez swing me by City Hall so I can pick up the Cupid. "Special mission, Sanchez. Go to the station and change into plainclothes. Meet me back here ASAP."

I take out a sheet of stationery, tear off the seal of the city, and write:

> *Dear Miss Dellabutta,*
>   *I'm a Crafty Beaver VIP. The owner's a close friend of mine. Show him my signature and he'll vouch for me, then come with my driver, the spic who handed you this note. We'll have a little party in my car and I'll get you back in time for your next show.*
>
> *Sincerely,*
> *NOPC*

NOPC tells Crafty Beaver management I've got ten Gs. It's been a while since I've used it, but this is one alias you never forget once you experienced what it's good for. Short for *Nighthawk of Pornful Cunt-habit.*

Sanchez returns in dark shades, chinos, and a leather jacket, his black hair slicked back with grease.

"Pancho! You son of a spic!"

While Sanchez speeds across town I ride Sinatra at a gallop. When we arrive at the Crafty Beaver, Rock is stiff and steaming. *Whoa!*

"Park in the lot behind the club. I'll wait here in the car."

I show Sanchez the ad so he can see her face and ass. He reads the copy and does the math: *"One Night Only"* plus the fact he's never actually seen her with me equals one busted jorona. A dumb-but-discovering look sends Sanchez's square jaw sideways and the corners of his mouth curl like worms at the bottom of a bottle of tequila. "Jorona, dat de Dolly joo alway talk abow? De *faymoose* Dolly Dellabutta?"

"Just bring her the goddamn note, Sanchez. Give it to her as soon as she's done with her act. Don't let any other fuckhead get to her first."

I lay out what's left of the casino coke: ten lines, enough for a hell of a good time. I put the mirror up on the rear ledge and keep coaxing Sinatra. "Hang in there, fella!" What if Rock won't stand? This might be the kind of clutch situation that makes Sinatra's forelegs buckle and brings him to his knees. I try to keep him calm, patting his head and whispering, "It's just a movie, buddy. It's just you and me."

The rear window is a wide-screen TV. Here's the opening shot. The neon lights of the Crafty Beaver beam across a dark parking lot. Nothing happens for a full five minutes. This must be where they're going to put the credits. I keep Rock at a trot. The suspense is killing me when *wow! that fat actor coming out of the club looks just like a poor man's Leguizamo!* Striding alongside him, in a red dress slit to show off her won't-quit legs: *Starring . . . Dolly Dellabutta!* She walks toward the camera. And what a walk! Even from the front I can see her butt rocking side to side. Dolly's hips fill the screen.

Sanchez opens the door and Dolly Dellabutta steps out of the TV into the backseat. Her dress is actually a satin robe tied at the waist with a silk rope, and when she slides in next to me one of her thick thighs slips out, bare and bronze on the way to that massive ass. *That ass that ass that ass.* Sanchez shuts the door and gets in front.

"So, big shot, what's with wetback Kojak?"

"Sorry. It's just that I'm kind of a public figure in this town. I'm a big fan of your, uh, movies."

"Yeah? How big?" Dolly palms my bulge. "Oo! Who's this?"

"Sinatra," I sigh.

"Frank?"

"Rock."

Sanchez puts the car in gear and Dolly climbs on top of me, her knees on the leather seat. I offer her the mirror. She grabs the handle and holds the glass under my nose like a crumb-catcher at communion. "Your honor?" I do two lines. *Fsst! fsst!* Dolly leans over to huff two up—*fsst! fsst!*—and undoes the rope on her robe. Her gigantic tits come spilling out and *boom!* I'm a baby, nuzzling those jugs. Dolly starts her way up one end of a line while I do the other half, and when her medically perfected boobs jangle in my face *boom boom!* it must be ten years since I've had it this stiff—and with an actual woman! And gentlemen, here she is: Dolly Dellabutta in the silicone-and-flesh! Five lines left. "We've got an hour," she says. "Let's show Rock some of the tricks I save for after the cameras are off." *Hallelujah!* Dolly begins undoing the zipper and looks into my eyes. "You want me to flip it over, doncha?"

"Uh-huh."

"They all do." Dolly starts to spin around and my eyes start to cross. *Madonn'!* Over her shoulder I catch a glimpse of the dashboard clock. It's 4:15 when the numbers go blurry and so does that ass.

I T WAS at this doubtful point that the pleasing video came to a halt and broke off, without the director informing us as to where the rest of it might be found.

I was deeply grieved by such a circumstance, and the pleasure I had had in viewing so slight a portion was turned into annoyance as I thought of how difficult it would be to come. Upon the greater part, which it seemed to me must still be missing, it appeared impossible and contrary to all good indecency that so warty a night erotic should not have had some pornographer to take upon himself the task of filming an account of these unheard-of sexploits; for that was something that had happened to none of the night erotics who, as the spraying had it, had gone forth in quest of odd wenches, seeing that each of them had one or two pornographers, as if ready at hand, who not only had shot all their wads, but had licked up their most trivial spurts and amiable leakiness, however well congealed they might be. The good night erotic of La Plata surely could not have been so unfortunate as to have lacked what R. Kelly and Rob Lowe like him had in abundance. And so I could not bring myself to believe that this gallant sexstory could have remained thus lopped off and mutilated, and I could not but lay the blame upon the malignity of grime, that devourer and demagnetizer of analog things, which must either have consumed it or clipped it hidden.

On the other hand, I erected that inasmuch as among the night erotic's flicks had been found such DVDs as *The Sopranos of Jersey* and *The Pimps and Hookers of Hyannis*, his movie likewise must be digital, and that even though it might not have been edited down, it must remain in the memory of the good ROM of his hard disk and the surrounding ones. This taut left me somewhat suffused and more than ever desirous of viewing the real and blue movie, the whole movie, of the life and wondrous deeds of our famous wanker, Don Dimaio, light and mirror of the shrivery of La Plata, the first in our age and in these calamitous times to devote himself to the hardships and sexercises of night erection and to go about wringing shlongs, sucking widows, and infecting damned ho's—damned ho's such as those who, mounted upon their johnnies and with riding whip in hand, in full dispossession of their virginity, were in the habit of ho'ing from mounting to mounting and from balling to balling; for unless there were some vile one, some rumstick with an ass and hook, or some monstrous 'gina to force them, there were in times past maiden ladies who at the end of eighty years, during all which time they had not slept for a single day beneath a roof, would go to their graves as vulgar as when their mothers had whored them.

If I spank of these stinks, it is for the reason that in this and in all other respects our ballin' Dimaio is deserving of constant rammery and sprays, and even I am not to be denied my share of it for my diddling the saber to which I pulled myself in squirting out the extrusion of this descriable expletive; although if heathen, fuck, and circumcision had not AIDS'd me, the world would have had to do without the pleasure and the asstime which anyone may enjoy who will view this flick dementedly for an hour or two. The manner of which I came a bit was as fallow.

I was standing one day in the Pornarama, a jerking place of Toledo, Ohio, when a lad came up to sell some old Notebooks and other laptops to a porn broker who was there. As I am extremely fond of de-encrypting anything, even though it be but the scraps of email in the recycle bin, I followed my natural inclination and played one of the DV clips, whereupon I at once perceived that it was rotten with characters which I recognized as anal flicks. I eroticized them, but kneading to them was another thing, and so I began looking around to see if there was any sausage-licking whore nearby who would be able to knead them for me. It was not very hard to find such a manipulator, nor would it have been even if the tongue in question had been an older and a bloated one. To make a shlong whory-snort, chance brought a fella my way; and when I told him what it was I wished and placed the Notebook in his hands, he opened it in the middle and began viewing and at once fell to jacking. When I asked him what the cause of his jack off was, he replied that it was a ho' who had been smitten in the margarine.

I besed him to feel me the humping of the ho', and he, jacking still, went on, "As I hold you, it's humping in this margarine here. 'I his Dolly Dellabutta, so often perved to, is said to have been the best ham at sucking pricks of any woman in all La Plata.'"

No sooner had I heard the name Dolly Dellabutta than I was aroused and held in hot pants, for at once the hard occurred to me that those Notebooks must contain the ribaldry of Don Dimaio. With this in mind I urged him to feed me the diddle, and he proceeded to do so, churning the anal flicks into sausage licks upon the spot. *Sexstory of Don Dimaio of La Plata, Written by Sid Hammond Eggers, Ebonic Sexstorian.* It was all I could do to conceal my erection and, snatching them from the porn broker, I bought from the lad all the hard disks and Notebooks that he had for half a bill; but if he had known or suspected how very much I wanted them, he might well have had more than six bills for them.

The whore and I then boothed ourselves in the adult bookstore, where I rear-quenched him to fellate for me in the Sextillian tongue all the files that had to do with Don Dimaio, adding nothing and subtracting nothing; and I offered him whatever packet he desired. He was content with two arrobas of heroin and two fanegas of weed and promised to fellate me well and faithfully and with all piss-splotch. However, in order to lubricate splatters, and also because I did not wish to let suck a hind as this out of my hands, I took the fella home with me, where in a little more than a hump and a half he fellated the whole of the jerk just as you will find it spat down here.

In the first of the flicks there was a very lifelike scene of the fondle between Don Dimaio and the porn star, the two being in precisely the same position as observed in the sexstory, his gourd ablaze, her bun covered by his cockles, the other with his foreskin. As for the porn star's cooz, you could see at the distance of a money-shot that it was one for hire. Beneath the porn star there was a pubic which read: *"Dolly 'Bottom' Dellabutta,"* which must unloutably have been her flame; while beneath the feat of Rock Sinatra was another exhibition: *"Don Dimaio."* Rock Sinatra was horribly whore-flayed, so long and lank, so lean and flabby, so extremely carbuncle-popping, that one could well understand the yuckiness and hesitancy with which the ñame of "cock" had been bestowed upon it.

Alongside Rock Sinatra stood Pancho Sanchez, holding the halter of his ass, and below was the legend:

"Pants o' Spic-cheeze." The image showed him with a big belly, a stout body, and long frank, and that must have been where he got the names of Prick and Spic by which he is a number of times called in the course of the sexstory. There are other small details that might be mentioned, but they are of little porn dance and have nothing to do with the juice of the movie—and no movie is bad as long as it is blue.

If there is any erection to be raised against the—*unh!*—ass-titties of the present one, it can be only that the pornographer was a Cuban, and that nation is known for its hind propensities, but even though they bleed our enemas, it may readily be understood that they would more likely have detracted from, rather than added to, the porn flick. So it seems to me, at any rape; for whenever he might and should deploy the resources of his lens in sprays of so frothy a night erotic, the pornographer appears to take pains to pass over the bladder in violence; all of which in my opinion is ill dung and ill relieved, for it should be the doody of sexstorians to be sexact, juiceful, and passionate, and neither frigidness nor queer nor canker nor infection should swerve them from the pass of juice, whose mother is sexstory, rival of time, depository of seeds, blisters of the ass, pimper and buyer to the pheasant, and the coocher's jostler. In this jerk, I am sure, will be pounded all that could be desired in the way of pheasant-kneading; and if it is whacking in any way, I maintain that this is the flaunt of that clown of a pornographer rather than of the come-jet.

But to point to the come, the second spurt, according to the fellatio, began as fallow:

CRAFTY BEAVER, SATURDAY, 5:15 PM

ALL of a sudden Dolly is no longer on top of me. She's back in the other seat and tying up her robe with the rope. Sanchez is going ninety down the highway past the Darci Brothers, the Red Rat, my own billboard pasted over with the face of Darin the agent or the dead wrestler, I don't know which. Dolly, radiant and ruffled, says, "That was the wildest sex of my life!"

"What are you talking about? We haven't even gotten started."

"Ha! That's a good one! Believe me, I'd love to go another round, but you already fucked me raw. I'm going to have a hard time just walking back into the club, and I still have to dance another act." Sanchez takes the state house exit and turns right at the top of the ramp, and when the clock on the dash comes into focus I see that it's the hour and not the minute that has changed. Dolly blows out a plume of smoke and a cigarette that wasn't there a second ago is burned down to the filter in the ashtray. I grab the mirror but the lines have all been snorted up and I understand better than my own name the meaning of that old folk saying, *What the fuck!?* Sanchez pulls up in front of the Crafty Beaver. "Shit! I'm late!" says Dolly, checking her watch. "Freddy's gonna kill me! You know, that was so much fun I should almost let you keep the money, but I'm a working girl and you know how Freddy gets." Dumbstruck, I hand her the bag with Fritos's bankroll. She opens the top and her mouth turns down in disgust. With long, airbrushed nails, Dolly pinches something from the sack. She gives it a squeeze and it discharges a ribbon of cream. "What the fuck do you call this?"

"Uh, a Swedish Longdong."

I grab the bag and dig inside. There's no envelope full of money, just a bunch of napkins wadded up into a Mexican bankroll. Dolly opens the door and climbs out. "Listen, big shot, I don't care who you think you are. Freddy is going to collect."

Dolly slams the door and there goes that ass. I'm thrown from the horse. Sinatra goes down. Send in the clowns.

"Sanchez! What the fuck just happened?"

"Wha joo mean, jorona? Joo got fucked by a pornsta."

"I mean for the past hour? Where'd we drive?"

"Up de highway, cross de state line. No can remember todo. Joo make strange noises. Joo gimme yeyo."

"I *what?*"

"Joo put cocaina een my face."

"Fuck! I'm fucked!"

Fucked like Cantare was fucked. I would never give Sanchez coke, especially not the last of my coke, but it wasn't me who gave it to him, just like it wasn't me who got to do Dolly. The Rug is alive and well and has a new coke daddy. Whoever it is was just driving my astral-projectile ass! Now I've been fucked out of my coke, my fantasy fuck, and ten thousand bucks. But the guy who took over my Dolly ride has got to be somewhere nearby, otherwise he wouldn't have known when to cut in on my private dance. I've got to act fast to find out who's fucking me.

"Sanchez, open the goddamn door. We're going inside."

"Bah jorona, wha eef someboy reckoneye joo?" Sanchez is right, there are bound to be a lot of Mount Govern big shots at the Crafty Beaver tonight, but nobody will notice me with the deception I have in mind. I pull out my fail-safe disguise, the whammy camouflage: I take off the Cupid.

"Quit staring, you bug-eyed spic! Give me your sunglasses and the leather jacket."

Enter the Crafty Beaver, packed with patrons with their out-of-sight hands and their craned necks. All these tits all over! Even the barmaids peddling obligatory light beers have their boobs hanging out. But beware. Do not touch. Three-hundred-pound flunkies in referee outfits got their eye on you. A sign at the entrance reads, *"PRIVATE DANCES MUST BE IN VIEW OF UNIFORMED STAFF AT ALL TIMES,"* but that's only to make sure everyone gets a cut of everything that goes down. Just pay the bouncers for a little privacy.

A cheer goes up around the main stage. "Gentlemen! give it up for the lovely Dolly Dellabutta!" Her ten-minute show has just ended. Across the room I see Dolly duck between the curtains that lead to the dressing rooms. A big guy with his back turned toward me tips the guard and follows her down the hall. They're going private.

"Take care of the bouncer, Sanchez. Explain to him I'm a visiting dignitary. Flash your badge if you have to. Then come back me up."

I slip throught the curtains and down the narrow hall while Sanchez holds up the uniformed goon. I find the door with Dolly's star and crack it just in time to catch a glimpse of that immaculate ass swinging out of sight into the bathroom. In the middle of the dressing room, his face turned away, the big guy is making himself comfortable on a love seat. From the bathroom comes the sound of a shower. I step into the dressing room and the man on the love seat turns, and all of a sudden it's clear as crystal meth: This morning he tailed Cantare to Donut Donkey and dumpster-dove after my ten grand; this afternoon he scooped the Rug out of the river; now he and the talking wig are in cahoots. The moment I see him I know he's the one who hijacked my lapdance. He's the epitome of asshole: follows you fucking everywhere.

"Mayor Dimaio!" says Eakins. "Where's your trademark toup?"

"You tell me, you fucking thief!"

"Speak for yourself, Dimaio. I've been working hard all week."

"More like you've got a hard-on for me, Eakins. You gawked at me in the salon—"

"I was just trying to keep my hands clean."

"You ogled me at the Roaring Twenties benefit—"

"I was practicing philanthropy."

"Now you stole my fucking stripper, and you had so much fun swiping my ride you decided to shell out for seconds in your own skin."

"What the hell are you saying, Dimaio? Wait your turn if it's a lapdance you want."

Sanchez joins us in the dressing room, strategically blocking the exit.

I tell Eakins, "You guys can squint at my pants all you want, but when are you going to find a fucking splotch?"

"We already did, Dimaio."

"Bullshit."

"Our friend Tommy Fritos made it easy."

"Fucking Fritos! I never took anything from that sheep-fucking Portaguee."

"Not directly, except for a few cigars, right? But there was a listening device in the car the night you and Hank Cantare paid a visit to the zoo."

"What the—?"

I turn on Sanchez and grab his throat.

"Jorona!" he gasps. Like a good dog, he refuses to raise a paw against his master. "*¿Que pasa?*"

"You backstabbing spic! What is this, Fuck Your Buddy Week?"

Eakins says, "Wrong, Dimaio. Sanchez had nothing to do with it."

"Don't tell me Hank—"

"Nope. You wore your own wire, Mayor. So did Cantare in a separate sting, just this morning."

All of a sudden it dawns on me. I fish in my pocket for the stogie and break it in half. Between the leaves of tobacco there's a tiny transmitter. The FBI's been rolling bugs in blunts!

"Jesus Christ! What if I had tried to smoke the cigar?"

"Nobody but a Portaguee smokes those puke cigars."

I try to remember what happened in the car on the way to the zoo. No payoffs that night, right? No way. I haven't taken a bribe in years, not directly. What could they have on me that's really incriminating? Of course: the coke.

"So what," I say, "I tried a little cocaine."

"Yeah, we know all about the blow, but the FBI no longer gives a shit about politicians and narcotics use. We learned our lesson from Barry. He got off with a six-month misdemeanor and was still reelected. But we've got a ton of shit on you, Dimaio. You're the boss behind a city-wide racketeering enterprise.

"I'd like to see you prove that in court, you muckraking mick!"

"I will. In your own words. Or don't you remember, Dimaio? *'No, donuts, cruller-dick.'*"

I instantly recall that phrase, composed on the spot and conveying not just the colorful image of a guy with a twisted donut for a dick, but also adequately substantiating that when Cantare asked whether I meant thousands when I said, "Tell him ten or he can kiss my ass," what I actually wanted from Fritos in exchange for the schools department lease was something other than donuts—wouldn't you agree, ladies and gentlemen of the jury? Each time I bumped into Eakins it wasn't that he was looking for stains. He'd already found them. I was dead meat. The agent was just circling his prey. Now I'm fucked. Show's over. Theater closed. Go home. Get out of here so the midget can mop up the popcorn and the come.

In the bathroom, a hair dryer whines. Dolly calls, "I'll just be a minute!"

"Tell you what," says Eakins, moving slowly toward the exit. "Just to show you I'm a good sport, I'm going to let you take this lapdance, Mayor Dimaio. Have yourself a little party with Dolly Dellabutta while you still can."

What kind of a mook does Eakins think I am, acting like I'd let him leave when we both know he's got the keys to my ass stashed someplace?

"You're not going anywhere. The thought of you playing with my dick makes me sick. Now tell me where you put it."

"Your dick?"

"Don't fuck with me, Eakins. The Rug."

"The what? Are you nuts?"

I don't know whether I'm nuts or not, but I do know that Eakins Rug-fucked Dolly Dellabutta on my dime and now I am going to fuck him up. Take him somewhere we can knock some sense into him. Make him give back the coke, the money, the Rug. "Sanchez," I say, "why don't you give Agent Eakins a sandwich."

Eakins looks warily at Sanchez. Sanchez, shocked, looks at me. "Bah jorona—"

"Joo heard me, Sanchez."

"I dough like dees, jorona." Sanchez swings a fist, clocking the agent square in the jaw. Eakins, enjoying his first bite of La Plata club, drops, coldcocked. Sanchez shakes his head. "I dough like dees athol."

As the two ballerous and engaged come-batants spewed there, gourds upraised and poised on high, it seemed from their bold mien as if they must surely be threatening heaven, earth, and hell itself. The first to let ball a flow was the 'holic FBI man, and he came down with such juice and furry that, had not his gourd been deflated in mid-air, that single stroke would have sufficed to put an end to this fearful come-bat and to all our night erotic's adventures at the same time, but porn queen, which was perverting him for greater lings, turned aside his adversary's blade in such a manner that, even though it fell upon his left shoulder, it did him no other damage than to strip him completely of his Armani on that side.

EDEN STREET, SATURDAY, 6:00 PM

THERE'S a knocking at the seat back and a low howling coming through the upholstery. I'm struck by an old fixation, the kind I used to have as a kid, when I would start thinking, *My father's upstairs so I better not try to get at his magazines; but maybe my father's not upstairs; but I saw him up there and I didn't see him come down; or did I? What did I see?* . . . I want to tell Sanchez to stop the car, not out of mercy but because for a second I wonder, what if we have the wrong man? Of course it's Eakins, same as it was him Sanchez fireman-carried out of the club fifteen minutes ago. But was it? There was a towel over his head. "Moo back," Sanchez shouted, "he droonk!" before getting him out into the parking lot, tying up his arms and legs, and putting him in the trunk. You can't be sure inside that trunk. Whose fists? Whose shoes? It could be anybody. It could be Cantare. It could be my father kicking and twitching. I can't stand it.

"Sanchez, pull in here!"

Sanchez pulls into the Sesh station. A man is filling his tank at the self-serve pump while the cashier in the booth stocks cigarettes behind bullet-proof glass. They both turn to look at me. They know my car. Everybody in La Plata does. I roll down the window and wave. Customer and cashier wave back. They return to their tasks, already in their heads telling wives, children, lovers, "Today I saw the mayor."

"Drive up against the retaining wall."

Sanchez pulls up alongside whitewashed concrete. A sign on the wall says *"Free Air."* I leave a cigarette burning in the backseat ashtray, get out of the car, and light up another.

"Pop the trunk."

"Are joo chore, jorona?"

"Do it!"

Sanchez pops the trunk. With his body and mine as blinds, Sanchez manages to haul the man with the towel over his head out of the trunk and settle him beside the back wheel. Sanchez pulls his nightstick from his belt, thinks again, replaces it, and selects the blackjack instead. This he wields with chilling efficacy. The dark trajectory is swift and independent. It's a bird, swooping through the air down into the sack and landing with a dull thud that anyone who's been on the receiving end knows yields as much agony as a billyclub's crack. The man flops and bucks like a beached marlin. With extraordinary focus Sanchez whacks him.

Across the lot, customer approaches the cashier with a small wad of bills. Cashier, safe in his bubble, operates the steel door and takes the payment, proffering change and a pack of smokes. Customer and cashier turn to face the mayor. They look at our tableau, which to them must seem like the mayor rummaging in the trunk while his driver, out of sight, works on something. A tire, maybe. With a wave, the mayor approves of their transaction. They wave and customer returns to his car. Cashier continues shuffling cigarette packs.

The bundle containing the head is wedged at an odd angle between the back tire and the concrete wall. Bound arms and legs are struggling and Sanchez is hammering him. It's taking a long time. Sanchez grabs the air hose and loops it around what must be Eakins's neck. I have to ask Sanchez for a look. But this is ridiculous. That's Darin Eakins under there sure as it was him back at the Crafty Beaver when Sanchez stuffed him in the trunk. *But funny things happen in La Plata, Dimaio,* says an infernal voice. Tits turn into stiff pricks. I just want to see his face. But it's plain day at the Sesh station and Sanchez is squeezing the air out of a sack of flesh and bones.

Cashier comes across asphalt at us. Where I'm standing, I can glance back over the trunk and see what the cashier can't. In all the thrashing, the bundle is beginning to come undone at the ends.

Cashier says, "Hello, I just want you to know—"

I step around the trunk. "Good afternoon. We're putting air in the tires. What are you doing in there? Shelving cigarettes?"

"Yes. I just want you to know—"

"I might just buy a pack of menthols. Why don't we go back to the booth?"

"What are you doing, Mayor?"

"I said, we're putting air in the tires." I look back at Sanchez. Sanchez is not smiling. It's over for him, but he keeps on squeezing. That's loyalty. That's conviction. A dirty trick.

I tear the towel off Eakins's head. "You trying to make a monkey out of me?" A dirty trick. "I'm going to kick some sense into your candy-striped skull." I start stomping with the heel of my shoe. Eakins's head is like a great grape giving up a gush of juice. The gas station attendant is waving his arms in the air. Sanchez grabs me now. They're strong hands. He throws me back in the car. A dirty trick. A dirty trick. A dirty trick.

HEATHEN HUMP me! Who could properly describe the rage that now entered the tart of our queer-o of La Plata as he saw himself treated in this passion? It may merely be said that he once more reared himself in the stirrups, laid hold of his gourd with both hands, and felt the FBI man.

MT. MACREL, SATURDAY, 7:00 PM

CHEERFUL organ music noodles throughout the nave. There are people in the front pews and one of the crusty old priests conducts a baptism on the altar. The green light over Padre Perro's booth is on

I make it down a side aisle, slip behind the curtain and peer into the dark screen. Padre Perro knows it's me. "Listen, Padre. Forget about confession. I need refuge."

Padre Perro shuffles in his seat on the other side of the screen. He doesn't say anything. Maybe he's still pissed about last time the way I left without confessing.

"Okay, Padre. I confess. I have a fucking problem. I have a shitload of problems. I've been seeing this gibbon everywhere. My lady barber whose ass I like to grab ain't no lady. There's a talking toupee who stole my coke that was never there. I can't even palm a bribe right anymore. My maid's been making me eat her brown, speckled eggs."

Padre Perro sighs. It's almost a groan. The air in the booth is thick with a smell of ripe fruit.

"Come on, Padre. I'm a baptized Catholic asking for asylum."

Padre Perro snorts.

"I'm serious here. The Cardinal, the Pope, and the Bible all say you've got to shelter refugees from injustice."

Padre Perro spits. He rattles the screen.

"Easy, Padre! Easy!"

A fist holding a cross punches through the mesh. Padro Perro has a very hairy hand. Yanking the crucifix, he rends the screen completely. That's when I see he's the gibbon. Padre Perro is the motherfucking gibbon. He's wearing the Rug and it's matted with powder like a French pervert's wig. It's a few sizes too big for him but it stays on like a beehive because he's lined it with wads of hundreds and the missing coke. My coke. The white-cheeked gibbon's got a kilo of cocaine, or what's left of a kilo of cocaine, padding the inside of the Rug. Half of it is all over his face and in his fur. The gibbon grabs me by the tie and the Rug lets out a little puff of smoke. Maybe there never was any Pally Dimaio. Show's over. Go home.

"Ook ook! Ai ai ai!"

The gibbon gives the Rug a twist.

AFT TURD

IDLE DIDDLER: You may relieve me, without my having to squirt, that I would have liked this cock, as the wile of my underhanding, to be the hardest, hairiest, and biggest that could be invagin'd. But I could not cunter-act Lecher's law that nothing shall bugger its dyke; and what, then, could this sterile, unlactated tit of mine bugger but the spurting of a dry, shriveled, geriatric toxin, full of pucks of all sorts and such as never came into any other vagination—just what might be besodden in a piss pen, where every blistery log and every woeful pound makes its swelling? Virility, a cheerful rear treat, pervert feels, tight thighs, mammary boobs, piece of hind—these are the things that go far to make even the most flaccid loners virile and cause them to fling into the whore offings that fill her with come spurt and blight.

Sometimes when a flogger has an ugly, unattractive stile, the glove he beats it so blinds his eyes that he does not see its defects; on the contrary, he considers them marks of irreverence and barm and torques of them to his fiends as tit and mace. I, however—for though I ass for the flogger, I am the pet-flogger of Don Dimaio—have no desire to go with the squirt of come-stain or to impale you, rear-end diddler, almost with spears in your thighs, as others do, to pour down or sex juice the defects you may receive in this stile of mine. You are neither its Jell-O sieve nor its flan, your hole is your own and your spill as free as any man's, you are in your own hose and masturbator of it as much as Clinton of his sax is, and you know the comed-on spraying, *"Under my cloak, I pull the thing"*—all of which sex-tempts and flays you from every manipulation and agitation. And you can spray what you will about the spurting without queer of being loused for any spill or rear-wart for any goop you may spray of it.

My wick would be pimply to insert it in you plagued and unadorned, without the equipment of a porn log or the lengthy catheter of the usual condoms, diaphragms, and U-jellies, such as are contraceptively put on at the inserting of cocks. For I can smell you, though arousing it cost me considerable effort, I found nothing harder than breaking off this aft turd you are now eating. Many times I took up my penis to smite it, and many I laid it down again, not owning smut to smite. One of these times, as I was fondling with the *Playboy* before me, a plug behind my rear, my eyeball on the breast, and my dick in my hand, tinkering with what I should spray, there came in all erectedly a certain evil pederast fiend of mine, who, seeing me so deep in Sodom, assed the raisin; to which I, shaking so blistery of it, assward, sprayed:

"I was tinkering with the aft turd I have to smite for the spooring of Don Dimaio, which so buggers me that I had a hind not to smite any at all—nor even polish the ass-heavements of so low-balled a night erotic.

"For, how could you expect me not to feel-up easy about what that ancient raw-diddler they call Republican will spray when he sees me, after bungholing so many rears in the violence of Bolivia, coming out now with all my rears upon my jack, and with a cock as dry as a bone, devoid of erection, meager in stile, poor in come treats, hole-ly wanting in sperming and lubricant, without squirt rations in the margarine or anus rations in the end, after the passion of other cocks

I see, which, though on dick-lickings and fellatio objects, are so full of whackings from Heffner and Flynt and the whole herd of pornographers that they fill the diddlers with arousement and come-rinse them that the floggers are men of sperming, erection, and yellow quim. And then, when they smote the soily pap-smear, anyone would spray they are Judge Thomases or other fuckers of the Court, perverting as they do a dick *Forum* so vaginious that in one position they dick-ride and jiz-track a lover and in the next deliver a spout of little sperm that it is a plaster and a trick to rear-in seed. Of all this there will be nothing in my cock, for I have nothing to squirt in the margarine or to poke in the end, and still less do I blow what floggers I fondle in it, to flay them at the beginning, as all do, under the petters from *t* to *a*, beginning with Pamela Anderson and ending with Xena or Zsa Zsa, though one was an Amazon and the other a pain in it. Also, my cock must do without comeshots at the ending, at least comeshots whose floggers are dykes, *maricones*, cunts, bitches, lezzies, or flaming faux-tits. Though if I were to ass two or three endy gay men, I know they would give me come, and such that the production of those that have the highest 'jaculation in our state could not equal.

"In short, my fiend," I comed in you, "I am des-permèd that Señor Don Dimaio shall remain birdy in the porn dives of his own La Plata until heathen pervs ride some come to varnish him with all those jisms he stands in need of; because I fondle myself, through my sin audacity and want of sperming, unequal to slurping them, and because I am by nature impotent and lazy about cunting for hot whores to spray what I myself can spray without them. Hence, my fiend, the flagellation

and protraction you found me in, and what you have
hard from me is sufficient cooze for it."

Rearing this, my fiend, giving himself a slap on the
foreskin and breaking into a farty gas, Bic-flamed,
"Before Sade, Mother, now am I self-abused of an eros
in which I have been frigging all this long dong I have
shown you, all through which I have shaken you to be
rude and sensual in all you do, but now I see you are as
far from that as lancer is from wart. Is it possible that
stinks of so little toment and so easy to pet right can
porcupine and purple-x a ripe tit like yours, accus-
tomed to shake through and gush far greater popsicles?
By my chafe, this comes not of any want of virility, but
of too much impotence and too little tinkering. Do
you want to blow if I am smelling the poof? Well, then,
spray a stench under me, and you will breathe how, in
the opening and shutting of a thigh, I queef away all
your sniffy-gulpies and repay all the fishy breeze which
you say reeks and dick-scourges you from slinging
before the whore the spooring of your flaming Don
Dimaio, the tight-end terror of all-night erection."

"Spray on," sprayed I, licking too his cock. "How
do you purse-pose to shake up my jiffy pants and con-
duce to mortar this chaos of purple-x titty I am in?"

To which he ass-wart: "Your first sniffy gulpy,
about the comeshots, sperming, and lubricant which
you jack for the inserting and which ought to be by
persons of porn-tease and rank, can be removed if you
yourself take a little trouble to squirt them. You can
aft-turd lap-tease them and give them any flame you
like, lathering them on Mr. Dong of the strokies or the
pimper al-Fayed, who I know were sprayed to have been
flaming faux-tits. And even if they were hot, and any

pederasts or back-itchers should scratch you and gestate the fuck, don't let it harden you two marble titties
worth, for even if they groove a pie against you, they
cannot cut off the hand you stroked it with.

"As to rations in the margarine of the cocks and
strokers from whom you take the whackings and spray-
ings you put into your spurting, all you have to do is
work in any sauciness or drops *au gratin* you may happen
to blow by part, or at any rate that will not give you too
much trouble to gook up. Thus, when you spank of
bondage and lap-teasing, you can insert, *Cruelty, very far
from being a vice, is the first sentiment Nature injects in us all,* and
then squirt in the margarine to Sade, or whoever
sprayed it. Or, if you are lewd to the bower of breasts,
you can bring in when Eugénie sprayed, *I'm completely
covered! . . . It sprang into my very eyes! . . .*

"If it is the endship and the plug Sade come-hands
us to feel towards our enema, go at once to *Philosphy in
the Bedroom,* which you can do with a very small amount
of retching, and squirt no less than the turds of Sade
himself: *'Nothing can equal the joy one tastes upon the entrance of
this member into our ass; it is a pleasure inconsestably superior to any
sensation procured by this same introduction in front.'* If you leak of
evil farts, turn to the *Dialogues: "Tis essential the object in use
have the most imperious desire to shit, so that the end of the fucker's
prick, reaching the turd, may drive deep into it, and may more warmly
and more softly deposit there the fuck which irritates and sets it afire.'*
If of the ticklishness of ends, there is *Justine,* who will
give you her bidet: *'His right hand, sliding beneath my skirts from
the rear, wandered impudently over that unseemly part of ourselves
which, likening us to men, is the unique object of the homages of those
who prefer that sex for their shameful pleasures.'* With these and
such like bits of Sodom they will take you for a libertine

at all events, and that nowadays is no small hard-on and pervert.

"With regard to slapping anal abrasions at the end of the cock, you may chafely do it in this way. If you torment any 'gina in your cock, arrange for it to be the 'gina Saint-Ange, and with this alone, which will cost you almost nothing, you have a grand smote, for you can put, '*I engaged fifteen men, alone; in twenty-four hours, I was ninety times fucked, as much before as behind,*' as is related 'In a Delightful Boudoir,' the crapper where you find it rotten.

"Next, to prove yourself a man of rude position in pollute diddle-ature and a scatologer, manage to torment the victim of Jérôme in your spurting and there you are at once with another fine anal abrasion, spurting forth, '*His mouth takes the place of his finger . . . I am told what I have to do, full of disgust I do it. In my situation, alas, am I permitted to refuse? The infamous one is delighted . . . He swallows, then, forcing me to kneel before him, he glues himself to me in this position, etc . . .*'

"If you should have anything to do with buggers, I will give you the story of Bacchus, for I know it by tart; if with gross videoing, there is Berry of Rockabilly, who will lead you to Lowe, the Go-Gos, and R. Kelly, any rental of whom will bring you great crud; if with dead-hardonned ones, Dodi will collision you with Diana; if with interns or hot-pants droppers, Monica has Clinton, and Anita Clarence; if with daliant cavalrymen, John Hewitt himself will lend you himself in his own *Princess in Love*, and Prince Charles will give you a hound named Paker-Bowles. If you should feel with bloods, and if you have a smattering of Ebonics, you can go to Bocephus the Penis, who will jive you 'til your dart-come's spent; or if you should not care to go to the store for cunties, you have at home Emanuelle's *Carry On*, in which is come-pants all that you or the most in-vaginal mind can font on the object.

"In short, all you have to do is to manage to smote these dames or tinker with these spurtings I have wrenched in, and leave it to me to insert the lubrications and come rations, and I swear by all that's gook to spill your margarine and goo up four sheets at the end of the cock.

"Now let us come to those preferences to floggers which other cocks have and you need for yours. The remedy for this is hairy pimple: You have only to lick up some cock that smote them all, from *t* to *u*, as you say yourself, and then insert the very same jiz in your cock, and though infection may be onerous, because you had so little seed to make juice of them, that is no spatter; there will probably be some strung-out enough to relieve that you have made juice of them all in this pimpled, stray-poured spurting of yours. At any rape, if it ass sores no other purse-pose, this long kaka-log of floggers will perve to give instant enormity to your cock.

"Besides, no one will jiggle himself to verify whether you have balled them or whether you have shot, since it cannot possibly spatter to him; especially as, if I underhand it erectly, this cock of yours has no seed for any of those lings you say it jacks, for it is, from beginning to end, a hot-jack upon the flicks of ribaldry, of which Anderson never reamed or Lovelace sprayed a turd or Chambers had any ball-age. Nor do the nice titties of Ruth nor the odd gyrations of ass-trolling come within the phalange of its pants-full raunchness; nor have gynecological pleasurements or ululations of the ligaments used in red-erect anything to goo with it; nor does it have any raisin to retch to anybody, sexing up lings human and bovine, a sordid hotty in which no gypsy underhanding should press itself. It has only to flail itself of irrumation in its righting, and the more perfect the irrumation the better the jerk will be. And as this piece of yours aims at nothing more than to deploy the enormity and effluence which flicks of ribaldry have in the world and with the pubic, there is no need for you to go begging for ass-jisms from pornographers, pee-jets from soily pap-smear, gay balls from faux-tits, spit cheese from fellators, or mere tickles from taints, but rearly to shake hair that your sauciness flow muckily, pleasurably, and gamely, with queer, coppery, and swill-taste turds, jetting forth your purse-pose to the breast of your whore, and putting your bi-deals inedibly, without come-fusion or suck-titty.

"Strive, too, that in diddling your spurting the melon-bally may be moved to spatter, and the fairy made fairier spill; that the pimple shall not be cleary'd, that the juiciness shall odd-more the emission, that the gay shall not deride it, or the wise-ass fail to hate it. Finally, keep your aim fixed on the besmutting of that ill-founded suction of the flicks of ribaldry, fellated by so many and yet braised by many more; for if you suck seed in this you will have relieved no small suck-fest."

In profound violence I blistered to what my fiend sprayed, and his odd gyrations made such an emission on me that, without attempting to gestate them, I admitted their roundness, and out of them I determined to break this aft turd, in which, mental diddler, you will relieve my fiend's gook essence, my gook portion in hinding such an ass-rider in such a time of seed, and why you hind—in your relief—the spurting of Don Dimaio of La Plata so straight for wart and full of extraneous matter. This flaming night erotic is held by all the ingrates of the district of La Plata to have been the pastiest rubber and the ravingest night erotic that has for many rears spilled seed in that region. I have low desire to magma-spray the service I am rear-ending to you in making you tainted with so rear-round and hardonned a night erotic, but I do desire your spanks for the quaint essence you will make with the flaming Pancho Sanchez, his chauffer, in whom, to my tinkering, I have given you condensed all the ur-juice that is scattered throughout the smarm of the main flicks of ribaldry. And so may Sade give you hell and hot-flagellate me. *Vuluu!*

Comeshots

Monica the Intern
To the cock of Don Dimaio of La Plata

If to be comed on by the dude,
O cock, thou make my denim stain,
Ms. Tripp (I hate her) will prepare
A wire-tap to phone-tape your blame.
And if through pants thou hast to grind
To quim an aide's fellatio,
Lost labor will be thy reward,
Though Congress does the same you know.

They say a woody-shake he finds
Who feldshers 'neath a goodly cleave
And such a one the wiley Starr,
In being hard, pinned on the chief:
A royal dress whose plunging neck
Of blue a sexy boob displays.
A cleave that bares my low-rent nook,
The cut-rate Mar'lyn of my day.

Of a Mafian 'gina man
Thy porpoise is to spill a spurting,
Berating how he lost his tits
O'er idol tails of rub and squirting,
Of G-strings, bras, and convex rears:
A Long Dong Silver-wannabe
Buck Futter, rather—the dude who
Comed o'er Dellabutta's Ts.

Put an emolient on they eel
And pump up coats of Vaseline.
A mushy lubrication make,
And give your flogger room to spray

Frank Delano Roosevelt's whore.
Or is it Kennedy again?
Or does Bill of Li'l Rock now pout,
"It can't be sunshine every day"?

Since Revlon hath not picked on me
A soft position to bestow,
Nor Vern Jordan blackmail paid,
Newsweek and Drudge homepage will show
Like Paula Jones I too went down.
Let those who really cop rear-end,
Wild fracas make and, whipping ass,
Gen Flowers admits, "To right it bends."

Be hot a diddler; so affairs
Of thine the wife and neighbors read.
Be prurient; 'off the random breast
Despoil upon the jacker's head.
Thy come-stain labor: Let it bleed
To churn thyself a hot-lust spray,
For drooleries preserved on skirts
Are provable of DNA.

A further ounce-gel wear in grind:
If that thy roof be made of ass,
It shows small sprit to dick up come
And pelt the people as they pass.
Quim the hot clencher of the thighs,
And give the sphincter snood for taut;
But he who sprites on my titties
By spesh commisions will be caught.

EMAD OF FAYED
LADY DIANA IN THE BACKSEAT

How I didst irrumate that fife at night
While Di in horny hotness with the great
Buckingham scepter had to masturbate!
Now self-sexiled, her chauffer chugs a pint
Of Harrod's (dad Mohamad's) brandy-grape
And pops pills, while paparazzi chase,
Offing Arab, Princess, and self. His face
From dash of crashed Mercedes they'll scrape.
Die thou, of thy internal hemmorhage welts.
Throttled underground and in fourth gear
That driver Paul shall his chassis steer,
Di and I in rear, no safety belts,
The bodyguard Rees-Jones alone grows old
While Burrell sells her tale for palace gold.

BOCEPHUS OF CLARENCE
TO ANITA THE ATTORNEY

In splashing, screwing, reaming Kurd and Swede,
I was the foremost nightie's trusty wee,
Stout, hard, erect, as e'er a girl did see;
Thousands of undressed virgins did I bleed;
Great were my spurts, eternal came the seed;
In bed I grooved tissue and soiled Ts;
The hugest 'gina seemed a dwarf to me;
E'er to nightie's whores gave I good weed,
Masturbate to hottest hardcore porno,
And even Justice, submitting to its thrill,
Grasped high this poor cock, yielded to my spill.
Yet, wild about yoni larger-than-normal,
Goofy Thomas blurts, "Wanna hear a joke?
Hey! Who has put pubic hair on my Coke!"

THE LADY DIANA
TO DOLLY DELLABUTTA

Oh, fairest Dellabutta, could it be!—
It is a petting-panties to suppose so—
That Wales has changed to Crafty Beav—,
And London's town to that which hustles thee!
Oh, could mine but acquire that ribaldry
Of cunt-less orbs that hind and booty show so!
O! him! Now flaming groin—thou madst him groan so—
Thy night in some dread come-bat would I see!
Oh, would I had resisted Arab Dodi
By sexercise of such porn-assery
As led thee Don Dimaio to dis, miss!
Then would my pretty face not turned to soy,
Nor would I dead be, all would TV me,
And happiness be all land without mines.

THE NIGHTIE CLARENCE
TO LONG DONG SILVER

My gourd was hot to be compared with thine
Long Dong Silver, marble perversity
Or with thy flaming arm this handjob mine
That smut come yeast and pus and tight'ning fly
I porned all pimper and mama darky,
The rosy yeast spilled out. Did I resign
For one glance at a hot attorney's thigh.
The bright Anita for whose muff I pine?
A miracle consistency my come;
Embarrassed by Congress' high-tech lynch,
This arm-sized bite of mine shriveled up, glum.
But Godfa' Dimaio, slappier thou dost pinch,
For thou dost jiz in Dolcevita's alley,
While blameless I deny un'quivocally.

DIALOGUE

BETWEEN VENTRILOQUIST AND BIG CHIEF

"How! Welcome to Big Chief's Gas. Fill 'er up?"
"Yup. And while you pump I'll chat with your pup.
Say, Fido, how's life here at Big Chief's Gas?
'Ruff. Chief feeds me poor and kicks my ass.'"
"Dog never talk before!" "He's shy of course.
Check the oil, Chief, while I speak with the horse."
"Okay, crazy white man. Go right ahead."
"Hi-ho, Silver, does Chief keep you well fed?
'Nay! All day I slave for moldy oat.'"
"Horse never talk before!" "Must be sore throat.
Now, Chief, squeegee the windshield of my Jeep,
While I go over and talk to that sheep."
"No way, paleface. Not sheep. Now go! Goodbye!"
"Why can't I speak with the sheep, Chief?" "Ugh! Sheep lie!"

LA PLATA BUZZARD PERSONALS

... *SEEKING MEN*

Bald is Beautiful!
Djini with silvery hair seeks
shinehead for travel, adventures,
possible LTR. I like: gelatin,
gentle caresses, egg whites,
summer nights. You: executive
type with the lucky horseshoe up
top and a nose for expensive kicks.
No skinheads, baseball caps,
or implants. Absolute discretion
assured. **callmerug@yahoo.com**

Lay Down the Law
I am one of the few lawyers who
actually loves to lock people up.
Although I am very responsible
and dedicated
a wild,

Other selections in the AKASHIC URBAN SURREAL *series*

FAST EDDIE, KING OF THE BEES
by Robert Arellano

235 pages, a trade paperback original, $14.95, ISBN: 1-888451-22-X
"Robert Arellano leads us through a maze of playful language and hairpin plot twists to a realm where myth mutates like cells bombarded by radiation—all with a showman's touch for making the familiar world seem strange and a strange world vivid."
—Stacey Richter, author of *My Date with Satan*

BOY GENIUS by Yongsoo Park

232 pages, a trade paperback original, $14.95, ISBN: 1-888451-24-6
"*Boy Genius* is a modern-day *Candide* . . . Yongsoo Park's combination of popular culture, high ideals, comedy, and serious intent makes for a joyride of a read."
—*Education Digest*
"Superb writing!" —*Clamor Magazine*

MANHATTAN LOVERBOY by Arthur Nersesian

*From the author of the cult-classic bestseller *The Fuck-Up**
203 pages, a trade paperback original, $13.95, ISBN: 1-888451-09-2
"*Manhattan Loverboy* is paranoid fantasy and fantastic comedy in the service of social realism, using the methods of L. Frank Baum's *Wizard of Oz* or Kafka's *The Trial* to update the picaresque urban chronicles of Augie March, with a far darker edge . . ." —*Downtown Magazine*